K.E. MONTEITH

Quitting my Boss

A WORKPLACE ROMANCE

Also by K.E. Monteith

<u>Standalones</u>
All Grown Up
Third Time's The Charm
One Dropped Key
Quitting My Boss
Gym Daddy

<u>Snowfall Valley Series</u>
Back When We Faked It
Strike to Burn
A Much Kneaded Union
Crushes & Christmas
Snapshot Problems
Dirty Charisma Check
Give Me a Redo

ASIN: B0B8XKVVPS

Amazon ISBN: 9798366686143

Ingram ISBN: 9798869385406

Cover design by: K.E. Monteith

Printed in the United States of America

For everyone who has trouble getting the right words out.

Please be aware, this book contains sexually explicit scenes not suitable for children.

Chapter One

Rachel

Two years ago

Morgan Bleckard, CEO of the largest chain bookstore in the Northeast, the hottest bachelor in the city, has the hots for me. Which was admittedly an egotistical thing to say given the fact that I'd only been working for him for a month. As his secretary. I mean, come on, the rich beyond-belief boss having a thing for his secretary? That was too stereotypical, too book-trope-y to be real. Except ...

"Rachel." I turned to face the man of all my recent hot dreams. He leaned against the doorframe of his office, the sharp lines of his navy suit shifting as he crossed his legs. Mr. Bleckard didn't say anything for a long moment, leaving me with no other choice than to stare at his full lips in anticipation. No one would blame me for thinking about how those lips would feel on my skin. Especially when I finally met his eyes and the light green was overshadowed by hunger.

Mr. Bleckard's eyes trailed down my body slowly, making goosebumps bloom. The man gave me goosebumps every damn time he looked at me like that. And he did it a lot. The other day, after I handed him the weekly manager reports, he tossed a crumpled sheet of paper towards the trash can. Towards. Not in, but right in front of. And then he asked me to pick it up on my way out. I could feel his eyes on my ass the whole time and it gave me a sort of ego trip. Especially when he made some sort of guttural noise when I bent over. I dreamt about that noise all the time now. Wet dreams … very hot, wet dreams.

Thinking of the dreams Bleckard inspired had me shifting in my chair and I crossed my legs, like that could keep the need pinned in place. But the action drew his gaze to my thighs, where my pencil skirt rode up. Bleckard's throat bobbed before he shook his head and returned to his office.

I don't know what compelled me to get up, probably lust if I'm being honest, but I did. I followed him into his office and stopped a few feet inside. "Did you need something, sir?"

Bleckard turned to face me and sighed. He paced the length of his glass desk, just one of the many modern pieces of furniture in his office that I pictured him taking on. The cold glass would make for a nice contrast to the heat of our bodies.

I bit my tongue and tried to drag myself away from the fantasies by looking around for something that couldn't be sexualized. Except there wasn't much in his office to distract me. No pictures, no decorations, no cup of colorful pens. The man was all business, all of the time. I wonder if he was just as bossy in the bedroom too. Shit.

Finally, Bleckard stopped his pacing and faced me, leaning against his desk. "Do you feel like you can say no to me, Rachel?"

The question caught me off guard. The words were delivered flatly but his hands were gripping the desk so tightly, they were turning white.

"Yes, sir. I mean, yes, I can tell you no."

Bleckard pushed himself up and took long steps toward me. Then he reached me and kept going. I stumbled back, my ass hitting the door and slamming it closed. One of Bleckard's hands braced against the door, the other took my chin and tugging until I met his eyes.

"I *need* you, Rachel. *Badly.* Yes?" Mr. Bleckard tilted his face down, his heavy breathing tickling my cheek.

"Yes." I don't know how I managed the word with his lips right there. He sucked a breath in, teeth sinking into his lips. Bleckard dropped his hand from my chin, grazing his fingertips down from my shoulder to my waist, which he took with a firm grasp. He pulled my hips to his and I gasped. Partly because of the sudden and bold move, but mostly because I was now pressed up against the hard bulge in his pants. A hardness that made my mouth water.

"Is there anything on the calendar today?"

I couldn't for the life of me remember a single thing that was on the calendar. But I could remember Bleckard explaining that he didn't take meetings on Tuesdays because Mondays were for fixing problems that happened over the weekend and Tuesdays were to catch up. Something about the logic stuck with me.

"No, sir." As soon as the words were out of my mouth, Morgan's lips were on me. He didn't start with my lips though, he started at my neck. Open mouth presses against my skin, sloppy and hungry and so fucking perfect.

For a second, the thought of Morgan being my boss and this being a bad idea crossed my mind. But what was the worst thing that could happen from a fling with my boss? Getting fired? I'd survive that. I wasn't exactly a secretary because it was my life long calling. And if how turned on I was right now was any indication, sex with Morgan would be worth it.

As Morgan's lips trailed their way up my neck, I fisted my hands in his jacket and pulled him closer to me. The fabric was so smooth, cool to the touch, and God, I wanted more. I shifted my weight to push against the door and wrapped a leg around his waist, keeping him pinned against me while I worked the buttons of his shirt.

Morgan smiled into my skin before sucking at my neck and drawing a groan from somewhere deep inside me, somewhere that hadn't been touched like this, ever. But it felt like too much too soon. Instinctively,

I stopped undressing him and put a hand over my mouth to muffle the sounds of eagerness. Morgan pulled back, taking his hand off the door to grab my wrist and pull it away from my mouth.

Morgan smiled into my skin before sucking at my neck and drawing a groan from somewhere deep inside me, somewhere that hadn't been touched like this, ever. But it felt like too much too soon. Instinctively, I stopped undressing him and put a hand over my mouth to muffle the sounds of eagerness. Morgan pulled back, taking his hand off the door to grab my wrist and pull it away from my mouth.

Oh, so that's how it was. Morgan didn't talk much. He spoke in simple, direct sentences. Apparently, he was saving all his talking energy for this. For saying things that made my cunt pulsate and my hips unconsciously rock into him. And apparently, that action had a similar effect on Morgan as his words did for me, because he let out a sound that vibrated through his whole body.

Then he finally took my mouth. And when I say took, I really mean it. One hand went into my hair, tangling and gripping tightly before tilting my head and bringing our lips together. He wasn't soft or slow, but all-encompassing and hungry. His lips, just as soft as I'd imagined, parted and his tongue glided over me. The move made me moan, parting my lips and letting him lick into my mouth. The feel of our tongues meeting was hot and twisting. The hand that remained on my waist slid down my thigh and back up my skirt to grip my ass. His hold was tight, gripping me with all the need I felt.

"These skirts have been driving me insane." Duly noted. That was the perfect excuse to buy every color and pattern available. His hand slipped under my panties, messaging my ass and rocking me into him. Yes, I'll definitely buy more of these skirts.

But then, just as my eyes rolled to the back of my head, he mumbled, "Don't wear them on Mondays. I need to get work done, for fucks sake."

Huh. Guess I don't need to buy more skirts after all. Bummer. But reasonable, I guess. We were technically supposed to be working. The line had to be drawn somewhere.

Morgan let go of my hair and started working my shirt buttons and my hands moved to do the same. Our wrists clashed, desperation making our movements sloppy and slow. When the frustration reached its boiling point, buttons went flying. Morgan stared down at my chest for a moment, nostrils flaring. I didn't think he noticed that I'd also torn open his shirt, until he leaned down to my breast, his lips brushing my skin, and murmured, "Order us new shirts on my card later."

"Yes, Morgan." The words came out breathy as his hands wrapped around my now bare waist and made their way up to my breasts. But he stopped when I'd said his name, fingertips just under my bra. His eyes had gone wide, the lust dulled by something else. Shock, maybe. Was I in the wrong to say his name? I mean, we were about to fuck and even if this wasn't something serious, saying his name shouldn't be a problem. Or did using his name remind him of our positions? Remind him that he was my boss and he shouldn't be fucking an employee, even one who was eagerly giving her consent.

"You can't do that, Rachel. It's too much. I can't handle it." His hands slid further up, pinching my nipples and drawing out a sharp groan. "Understand?"

"Yes, sir."

That shouldn't have been my answer. I should've stopped right there. If a man wasn't gonna let me scream his name during sex, then I shouldn't be fucking him. But I wanted Bleckard so badly. And it's not like I was looking for something serious right now anyways.

Bleckard abandoned my breast, undoing his buckle and zipper and pulling out his thick and impressively hard cock. Drool pooled under my tongue as he rubbed against me. His hands returned to my thighs, running up until his fingers reached my panties, pulling them aside and sliding a finger over my clit. His cock twitched against my leg as he slid his finger into my pussy, curling until I screamed for him.

"So fucking wet for me."

"Yes, sir."

And from there on I was a fucking goner.

Chapter Two

Rachel

Present day

There was less than three weeks until I turned 30 and the only thing anyone seemed to say to me these days was, "Isn't it time you take things more seriously." More seriously as in settle down with a man, start thinking about children, quit being a secretary, and, if any of those judgemental assholes that called themselves friends knew, stop fucking your boss.

And I kinda had to agree with the last one. I mean, I'd been fucking Bleckard for two years, nearly every workday. And what had I gotten out of it besides exciting sex and countless orgasms? Nothing.

Well, obviously the orgasms weren't nothing. Most of the men I tried to date looking for that elusive man who would make me want to get serious couldn't even give me that. And I never regretted letting Bleckard fuck me whenever and however he wanted, not once. That man's body did things to me. And the way he took me so often made me feel like he was just as addicted to my body as I was to his.

But *that* was the problem. The only thing we did, outside of work, was fuck. We didn't have any friendly conversations, no subtle flirting by the water cooler, nothing. And that was fine, great even when after the first time we fucked and I was worried about what would happen next. But when I thought about the kind of man I wanted to get serious with, the kind of man I hoped to fall in love with, the kind of man who would give me the intimacy I was missing, this wasn't it. Especially since I still couldn't bring myself to say his first name. I was still a little bitter and embarrassed about that bit.

So if I wanted to meet any of the stupid expectations of my mother and others, and still be wrinkle-free in my wedding photos, and not give in to the a spiralling panic attack about my future loneliness, I needed to cut myself off from Bleckard. That and get serious with the one man I'd met who seemed like the perfect fit.

Greg Hall was perfect ... on paper. He was sweet, always held open the door, had a good relationship with his parents, asked me about my day, and was just an overall good guy. And he even humored me whenever I asked to take pictures for Instagram. The sex though ... just didn't hold up to Bleckard. But I was pretty confident that would get better once I'd quit my boss, fucking him and working for him. Plus emotionless sex seemed like a bad reason to not go after something that could bring me actual happiness.

I took a deep breath and hit print on my resignation letter. As the letter was inked out line by line, I chewed at my lip. The letter wasn't exactly personal. In fact, it was almost entirely a copy of the first resignation letter I found online. It was bland and cold and kind of reminded me of the man I needed to hand it to. My stomach twisted.

This was fine. I was just nervous because I was quitting my job. It was a big move. Totally natural. It had nothing to do with the other circumstances surrounding my decision. There was no doubt in my mind that this was going to lead to a better, more fulfilling relationship in one way or another. But that twisting feeling didn't exactly fade with reassuring logic. And ...

The paper, fully printed, fell to the floor and I cursed under my breath as I bent over to pick it up. And while my head was down, I heard Bleckard's steps walk past. He didn't pause to see what I was doing or speak, but he did leave the door open when he went into his office. And normally that meant I would follow him inside for my earth-shattering orgasm of the day. And damn, my body really liked the sound of that. I could already feel heat bubbling at my center, demanding attention.

But not today, body. Greg will take care of those needs when I see him tomorrow. Probably.

I grabbed the paper and quickly stood. Nervously, I ran my hands over my clothes, smoothing out wrinkles and readjusting my skirt length. When I was satisfied with my clothes, I started picking at my nails. This week's color was a dark plum. I had hoped that having my favorite color on me would help ease some of the tension of this moment.

From his office, Bleckard cleared his throat.

Right, he'd probably heard me get up and was wondering why I wasn't already climbing onto his dick.

Well, that's not true. Bleckard didn't skimp out on foreplay. In fact, he was probably wondering why I wasn't splayed out for him and …

Nope, no more stalling. No more thinking about fucking Bleckard. It was time to do this.

So, shoulders back and head held high, I strode into Mr. Bleckard's office and set the letter on his desk. And then took a step back. And then another because his scent made my body melt and I was having none of that today.

Bleckard's hands, which had been clutching the arms of his chair to the point of whiteness, moved to pick up the sheet of paper. His jaw tensed as he read, but there was no other change to indicate how he felt about the news. You'd think after two years I'd be able to read his emotions a bit more. But even after all the sleep I lost wondering how this moment was going to go, I didn't have a fucking clue.

"Rachel, is it April 1st?"

"No, sir. It's barely March."

Bleckard stood from his desk so quickly that his chair slid back into the wall. The crash made me stiffen, but Bleckard paid it no mind as he took slow steps towards me, eyes still on the letter in his hand.

"Then what kind of joke is this? 'Please accept this as my formal notice of resignation.'"

"It's my … resignation notice, sir. I … don't know what else to say."

"Maybe the reason you want to leave." Bleckard stopped in front of me, the cedar or whatever woodsy scent he wore having a wobbly effect on my legs.

"I'm quitting for personal reasons, sir."

Bleckard's brow furrowed and his chest rose with sharp breaths. "And I'm not entitled to know about your personal life?"

Shit, I wasn't prepared for this. This was supposed to be simple. There weren't supposed to be hurt feelings, there were no feelings to begin with. Where was this coming from?

ng from? "Sir, we're not even on a first-name basis. We barely know each other." Why did his reaction make me feel so guilty? The lines of our relationship were drawn, *by him*, a long time ago. We didn't even have a relationship, not really.

"What basis are we on then?" Bleckard took another step, letting the paper fall to the floor and taking my waist to pull me against him. "Because I've memorized the feel of you coming on my cock."

The goosebumps spread across my arms like wildfire. Bleckard noticed and pulled me tighter. My brain was short-circuiting trying to follow this conversation, trying to figure out how it got so out of hand so quickly, trying to decide if this meant I was making a mistake or not.

"Tell me what basis we're on, Rachel? Or do I have to fuck it out of you?" One hand shifted to my thigh, fingers sliding under my dress and pushing up, up, up.

"Morgan, stop."

His hands froze. And when those bright green eyes met mine I finally found an emotion I could read. Confusion.

"There's someone else that I'm seeing, someone I'd like to get serious with. So this–" I stepped back so his hands fell off me and gestured between us. "Whatever this was, it's done. I'm quitting. I didn't think you'd care since we aren't even dating."

His hands were still frozen, held out as he stared down at them in disbelief. God, what had I done wrong this time? Why was he so confused? What about this did I get wrong?

"You think we're not dating?"

"Well, I don't see you outside of work, we don't go on dates."

"Are those necessary?" Bleckard's brow furrowed. He finally drew his hands back, fisting them into his pockets.

Was I speaking a foreign language? Did this man really think we'd had some sort of relationship beyond sex? And then there was also the fact that he did go on dates, just not with me.

"You go out with those other women."

"You mean the women my mother is friends with?"

"Friends? Funny your mom is friends with a lot of hot, young 20-year-olds." Bitter, I sounded bitter. And I wasn't. We weren't in a relationship that would justify any bitter feelings. But if he considered us dating, how the hell would he justify going out with those women?

"I don't know what you're implying, but I didn't consider any of those dinners dates. Why else would I have had you arrange them?"

"I don't know. To remind me our relationship isn't serious. Or maybe just because it's part of the job. I don't know. I didn't question it."

"And you think I fucked those women?" Bleckard winced at his own words.

"Yes." I felt like I was losing my mind. Had we been on completely different pages this whole time? Did it even matter at this point? Or was this just proof we both needed to move on from each other?

"And so you've been fucking other men? I can't imagine how you have the energy for it after … us."

"You may fuck me often, sir, but my sexual appetite isn't exactly satisfied by quick fucks in your office. And I … I was under the impression that our relationship wasn't serious, so yes, I fucked other men, I dated around. I looked for the emotional connection you didn't … I didn't think you wanted."

"You never thought I was serious about you?"

I wanted to slam my head against the wall. Why the hell would I consider this man for a serious relationship? None of his behavior made me think he was even interested in a relationship, let alone a serious one. This man had fucked me on every surface of this room, during business calls and everything. We weren't some sweet little rom-com, we were straight-up erotica.

"Sir, the first time we were together, you told me not to say your name."

Bleckard's throat worked, but he didn't say anything. And shit, something about that really hit me. Because Bleckard wasn't the kind of man who held his tongue, at least not based on what I knew about him. Sure, he didn't talk a lot. But that was by choice. That throat thing made me think he was holding something back. He had really thought we were in some sort of relationship. And I just trampled all over that. And that felt like shit.

"I'm sorry. For the misunderstanding, sir. It seems like we made different assumptions about what was going on between us. And that — I'm sorry." I took a deep breath and tried to formulate more words, which was getting very hard. I felt guilty, but at the same time, I wanted to shout that he was just as guilty for … whatever was happening. I didn't exactly assume he wasn't serious after a series of dates or long walks on the beach. He didn't talk about his emotions, regarding me or anything else. *He* didn't initiate that clarifying conversation either. And if he tried to blame me, I'd flip. "But in this case, my leaving is probably the best for both of us. So if you'll excuse me, I'll get things filed with HR."

I turned to leave but froze when I heard Bleckard's footsteps behind me. He took hold of my wrist and tugged gently until I was facing him. I still couldn't read his expression. His brow was furrowed, either in irritation or concentration. I couldn't tell.

"Don't quit."

"Sir, given … everything between us and the fact that I intend to pursue another relationship, I don't think that'd be good for either of us." I tried to keep my voice light. Like I found out all the time that the guy I was banging on a regular basis considered us more than just fuck buddies. But his grip on my wrist tightened, not painfully, just a pulse of compression.

"That man you mentioned … do you love him?"

"I …" I didn't want to lie to him. Even though that would probably end the conversation right away. But I couldn't help but tell the truth. "I think I will."

His hand tightened around my wrist again and then he let go and stepped back.

"Then there's still time."

"Time? Time for what?" Was he talking about when I'd leave? I'd put in the letter, which was still on the floor, that I'd work the standard two weeks.

"For me to prove to you that I'm serious about us."

Chapter Three

Morgan

A year ago

Conferences were the worst part of my job. It meant being on my feet all day, being crowded into rooms that were always too hot or too cold, and being bombarded by conversations I had zero interest in. The only saving grace of this event had been Rachel accompanying me. And even that had been spoiled by some man who was now following us from dinner to the hotel, blathering on about his company's printing speeds. He'd sat down at our table earlier without invitation, just as my hand had started sliding up Rachel's skirt, and hadn't let up since.

As we crossed the lobby floor, the man stayed at my side, still talking about something I'd long since lost track of. Did he plan to follow us all the way up to our rooms? Behind me, Rachel followed, ever the perfect assistant alongside being the perfect woman. From a professional perspective, she'd done outstanding; even better considering this was her first conference. All her notes from the panels were neatly typed and organized, along with any contact information we received while walking around. As her boss, I was more than grateful I wouldn't have to waste my time tracking down new contacts. But as her partner, I was more concerned that she had a relaxing evening. And perhaps a little reward in bed too. Having her in a bed for the first time had been the only thing I looked forward to for this trip.

When we reached the elevators, I finally turned to the man, my patience at its limit. "You'll have to excuse us, we're done with business for the evening."

The man stammered, eyes shifting between Rachel and me, concern paling his expression. I truly couldn't comprehend where his confusion came from. And I wasn't inclined to educate him on where he'd gone wrong.

"Oh, yes, Mr. Bleckard, I was just hoping that we could –" the man stumbled over his words, only stopping when Rachel stepped up and cleared her throat. After six months of seeing her almost every day, touching her nearly as often, you'd think I'd get tired of looking at her. But I hadn't. Even the tight smile she offered the man was a welcomed sight. I should be concerned about the fact that I couldn't get enough of her. It should frighten me that she was the only one whose company I actively sought out. And it did. It reminded me of moments in my childhood when Mother would call me clingy or needy, saying that it wasn't behavior appropriate for a man. And like hell I'd let Rachel see me like that and risk her pushing me away or hating me. As long as I could control myself, things would be fine.

"I'll take your card, Mr. Lockley, and we'll reach out when we're back in the office." As always, Rachel picks up after my deficiencies. She accepts the business card the man offers, ignoring how his stutters went from intimidated to awkward as he ogled her. I didn't have the grace to ignore the action, though I knew I should. The growl that came from deep within my chest was involuntary. So was the twisting in my gut.

Lockley stiffened in response, quickly muttering farewells before scurrying off. And Rachel ... she raised an eyebrow but didn't comment on my unseemly behavior. Good. I couldn't bring myself to vocalize how much I didn't like the way Lockely looked at her. It was embarrassing and unnecessary.

The ding of the elevator saved me from having to address the issue and we had a silent, but comfortable ride to our floor. As the inane chatter from the lobby fell away, my shoulders began to relax. I took the moment to eye Rachel over. She was leaning against the wall, eyes closed, feet shuffling so that her heel slid in and out of her shoe. She was tired. I cursed myself for not expecting it. Of course she was tired. We'd been walking all day, working all day. And this was her first conference. I was an idiot for having any expectations for the evening. Rachel needed a night of relaxing, not me fucking her till she was sore.

When the elevator doors opened to our floor, we stepped out and paused there. Rachel looked up at me, head tilted, a curious glint in her bright brown eyes. But that glint didn't outweigh the tiredness. So instead of asking for what I wanted, her in my bed until morning, whether or not we planned on fucking, I fished the extra key card for my room out of my pocket and handed it to her. "Wake me tomorrow morning, please. Six o'clock."

Rachel looked at the key for a short moment before her eyes met mine, a brow raised. *Ask me.* It felt like I was begging, like I was on my knees. That's what my want for her did to me. *Ask me to take you back to your room, mine, whichever. Ask me to ravish you, to warm a shower for you and ease the weariness of the day away before I made you forget your name. Ask me. Anything. I'll do it.*

"Understood, sir." Rachel nodded, slipping the key into her bag before turning away and heading to her room. I stood there, watching her safely enter her room before my breathing returned to normal.

Good. This was good. She'd needed the rest. And even though we'd been working, we had spent the last several hours together. It should have been more than enough. Anything more would have been clingy. It's not like I'd ever felt the need to spend the night with my previous partners anyways. This should be no different.

But fuck, it was.

The curtains at this hotel were cheap, flimsy pieces of shit that let morning light drift in unfiltered. And though I knew I should just get up and start my day, knew that I wasn't going to get any more rest, I kept my eyes closed. Because Rachel had said she would wake me and for some unfathomable reason, I wanted her to be the first thing I saw this morning.

A beep sounded from the door followed by the click of it opening and my pulse quickened. Soft footsteps made their way into the room, then stopped. Stopped too far away. My brows furrowed, ears straining to pick up on whatever it was Rachel could be doing.

Maybe she didn't want to do this. Maybe she had no interest in waking me up. It wasn't something I had asked or done for my previous partners, but with Rachel, I —

"Fuck." The word came out as a hissed whisper as the sheets were pulled away, cold air prickling my skin. But that sensation was quickly replaced by heat as Rachel's hand palmed my morning wood. My cock quickly stood to attention under her touch, straining against the fabric of my underwear, desperate to get more of her. Rachel hummed and when I opened her eyes, she was settling onto the bed, legs straddled over one of mine and head tilted down towards my cock with a look of hunger. She knelt down, one hand sliding into her dark curls, pinning them back, and the other tightening around the waistband of my underwear. She paused there, licking her lips before looking up at me. There was a small drop of drool teasing the corner of her lips, a sign of desperation that matched my own.

I didn't care that this wasn't how I'd pictured my wake-up call. I didn't care that this would make us late or hurried. All I cared about was getting a piece of this woman, just a scrap, just enough to last me the rest of the day. Something that would fulfill this seemingly endless need.

I nodded and Rachel immediately pulled at the fabric, tugging it down just far enough to free my cock. She dropped her hold on my underwear to take a tight grip around me, stroking until I fully thickened for her. And when I had, she leaned further down, resting a gentle kiss on my crown.

The tenderness in that act rubbed at something raw inside me. Something that should be addressed. But not now. Not in front of her.

So instead, I slid one hand into her hair, our fingertips meeting, pinning back the curls, and guided her to take more. Her lips parted over me slowly, gliding down with ease. Then she pulled back, her tongue tracing zig-zags up my cock. My grip on her hair tightened as she went back down. And when she began to suck, cheeks hollowed and drool dripping down my shaft, my eyes rolled back.

"Fuck." It seemed the only word I was capable of when my girl was sucking me off. I forced my eyes back open, not wanting to miss the sight of her. Rachel let go of her hair, her hand dropping to caress my balls. But her curls fell in front of her face, blocking my view. And I just wanted to see her. I grunted, the sound involuntary, and used my free hand to hold the rest of her hair back. Brown eyes met mine, brow quirked. She seemed to see the answer to whatever question she had and nodded, returning to bobbing up and down my cock.

There were too many details about this moment I wanted to remember. The way Rachel's nostrils flared as she took slow breaths before going further. The dark green of her nail polish as her fingers slid up and down. How her curls weren't as tight as usual. There was nothing in the world that could tear my eyes away from her. Nothing but the intense pleasure she created that made my eyes roll to the back of my head.

"Stop," I gasped, tugging gently on her hair, desperate to avoid the oncoming relief until Rachel got hers.

"On my face." The words came out as a growl instead of the desperate plea they were. Rachel let herself be pulled away, but her eyes remained on my cock as she let one hand go to wipe away small lines of drool on her chin. Eventually, she nodded and sat back. My fingers slipped through her hair and I missed its silken touch. But then Rachel leaned back down and kissed my head again, a quick peck before crawling off the bed. It was for the best that her mouth was off of me, a second longer would have ruined me, but watching her shift at the foot of the bed, out of reach, was just as torturous.

I sat up, leaning forward to pull her closer and help push her leggings down. I don't know why she had them on in the first place if this was how she planned on waking me up. She should know by now that I couldn't let her have me without also getting a taste.

Pants discarded, my hands rested on her waist, reveling in the soft touch of her skin, the give of it. But hunger gnawed at me and I gave into it. I tugged at Rachel and she followed, crawling over me as I laid back down. But when she shifted to straddle me, she was facing away, body tilting forward toward my pelvis.

"You're done sucking my cock, Rachel." I shifted my grip on her so that I could spin her around and pull her pussy where I needed it. "It's my turn."

Rachel huffed above me and I narrowed my eyes at her, hands digging into her ass. I tried to find the words to describe how badly I needed to taste her without sounding like the needy bastard I was. But she relented, settling her knees on each side of my head and lowering just enough so that she hovered over my mouth. I took a deep breath first, soaking in the scent that drove me absolutely insane. Rachel shook, leaning forward to grip the headboard. Her knees shuddered before sliding apart and finally setting her weight upon me, covering my mouth with her delicious wetness. My mouth watered instantly and I had to drop one hand from her ass to my needy cock. I squeezed the hard flesh, slick with the evidence that Rachel enjoyed putting her mouth on me the same way I did.

"I want you to fucking drown me, understand?"

Rachel's mouth opened to respond but the words were cut off with a gasp as I began to lick her. Long and slow, savoring the taste. I'd just barely finished my perusal of her lips when she started to grind against my face. Her clit rubbed in small circles against my nose and I pushed into her, desperate to give her what she needed. I slid my tongue inside her, pushing against the edges of her cunt. Rachel shook above me, some sort of plea muttered under her breath. Good. I quickened my pace until I found the rhythm that had her shuddering, one hand falling from the headboard to twist into my hair. Then I pulled at her hip, nudging her down so her clit landed on my lips. And I sucked. Two sharp pulls then three swirls of my tongue, just the way she liked. Over and over again until she came, her taste flooding me with pleasure and her knees pinning me in place as she rode that high. Looking up at her, forehead resting on the arm she braced against the headboard, I was stunned by the image of her. Perfection. My woman was utter perfection.

And I needed to be inside that perfection, *now*. Without me saying a word, Rachel read my need. She shifted down until her pussy rested on my cock, rocking herself up and down my length. And then she leaned down, kissing my cheek and licking up the mess she'd made. And that action made me feral.

"Sir, we need to leave soon." Despite her word, her voice shook as she continued to slide her swollen clit against me.

"Then I suppose I should get you back on my cock then." With a tight grip on her hips, I shifted our weight and swapped our positions. The gasp she made pulled the edges of my lips up. I guided her legs up my waist, pulling her hips so she was angled up, open and ready for me to bury inside her.

I loved this view of her. I loved every view of her. But *this*, this clear and irrevocable proof of her desire, her need for me. I didn't get to enjoy the view for long though, because Rachel reached between us and guided my dick inside her.

"Worried about our flight or are you just impatient today?" I didn't let her answer, didn't want to chance hearing something I didn't want to know. Instead, I pushed into her, hard, drawing a gasping scream from those gorgeous lips.

"Let's see if we can get the front desk to call us about a disturbance."

Rachel wrapped her arms around my neck, kissing and sucking and muffling her whimpers into my skin. The warmth of her mouth burned and I could do nothing else but pound into her, marveling at the way she clung to me in every way.

Being inside Rachel simultaneously calmed every nerve in my body and lit them all ablaze. And suddenly the constant noise, the endless lists of things to do, and thoughts to hold back were gone. There was just Rachel. The way she pushed up into me. The way her ragged breath and whimpers heated my neck. The way her fingers dug into my shoulders and heels into my ass. Perfect. My girl was perfect.

"Sir." My attention refocused on Rachel under a different light, searching for that final push she needed to come. And she needed to come soon because that heat she spread in me was quickly coming to a head.

"Kiss me."

Rachel pulled back, sinking her fingers into my hair, and did exactly as I asked. If I was a better man, I'd sacrifice the angle to worship her clit. But I wasn't a better man. I was a man desperate for every gasp she made when I sunk deep into her. Desperate for the way she shook against me. Desperate to have her lips on mine while it was appropriate.

"Get your hand down there. Otherwise, we'll have to continue this on the plane." My cock twitched inside her at the idea, the excitement, and Rachel had a similar reaction. The way her pussy pulsed around me as she quickened to follow my instructions made me want to pull her hand back, stop while we were both desperate and aching, make us wait till we're in the air and the fasten seatbelt signs go off. But she was close. Her fingers slid between us and moved in tight circles over her clit. Her nails scratched against my skin and I couldn't bring myself to pull away. The sting was what I needed. *She* was what I needed.

Rachel's grip on my hair tightened. Her kisses paused, lips resting on mine, parted with heavy pants. And the warmth of her orgasm became the becoming of mine. The moment was blinding. The heat that coursed through me and the thundering of my heart was nearly overwhelming. But it was perfect, having her in my arms, feeling her shudder, feeling her breaths settle from ragged to calm. That's what this moment after was, calm.

"We ... we need to get going, sir," Rachel said. I grunted an affirmative and moved off her. Ridiculous. I was being ridiculous. When had I ever wanted to hold someone after sex, have them cling to me like a raft? That was obsessive, clingy shit. Rachel would hate a man like that.

Chapter Four

Mogan

Present day

"If I can't prove I'm the one you should be with within two weeks, then you can quit without notice."

Remembering the desperate words I'd said to Rachel earlier made me cringe. Though it was hardly the worst part of that conversation.

The worst part was finding out that everything I had ever thought about our relationship was a lie. No, not a lie, just something I'd built up in my head and my head alone. We were just two people who enjoyed each other's bodies and nothing more. Nothing more. These past two years while I considered her mine, she hadn't even considered us dating.

My grip on the steering wheel tightened, fingers going white. I ordered myself to take a deep breath, that I would have this all figured out by the time I got home. Home, where the few pictures I had were of Rachel and me at various company events over the years.

My breath came raggedly. I was losing it. Losing her.

No, that wasn't a productive line of thinking. And I needed to be productive when it came to Rachel. She'd been willing to leave me, quit her job, with no conversation, all for some man she wasn't even in love with.

This time I succeeded in taking a deep breath.

I just needed to start at the beginning and unravel things from there. That's how I was able to solve all my work problems, that's how I'd solve this. First I needed to think of everything from her point of view and see where I went wrong so I could make it right.

The first time we met was for her interview. I'm fairly certain I didn't say much to her other than a greeting and a farewell. I couldn't have made much of an impression. But she made one on me. She'd answered my previous secretary's questions quickly, a soft smile lighting up those bright brown eyes. Unlike all the other candidates, she didn't flutter her eyelashes at me or fiddle with her hair. And she didn't avoid looking at me either. Most people, when they know who I am and that I don't care to talk, get the idea that ignoring my presence altogether was what I wanted. Rachel didn't do that. When my name was said, she looked at me, waited for a beat to see if I had anything to add, then looked back. She acknowledged me, saw me in a way most people didn't.

And yes, I found her insanely attractive. Looking at her made my blood boil, made the desire course through me so thoroughly that I'd thought I'd explode without warning. But it was that first thing that made me hire her. The attraction was secondary, something I had no intention of acting on. Especially since during the interview, she gave me no indication she saw me as anything other than a potential employer. I was resigned to that fact before the job offer was made.

But then she started. And my workload was suddenly lighter. And I couldn't take my eyes off her. Off those skirts that rode up with every step. Off the neatly organized reports she handed me. Off the door that separated us throughout most of the work day. And it drove me insane. I resort to childish tactics, like purposely missing the trash can when I threw something away, just to keep her in the room with me longer.

A month in, I found myself stepping out of my office with no reason but to see her. I called her name and she looked at me, confused but also like she was contemplating the same things I was. Like she was wondering what it'd be like to kiss me. And because I still had some common sense left in me, I returned to my office without a word.

Except she followed. She followed me and asked what I needed. Her breath had been heavy, goosebumps spread across her arms, and that skirt. I broke. I asked for what I wanted, I asked for *her*. And she said yes.

But apparently, she was only saying yes to sex, not a relationship, not exclusivity, just sex. And that thought was reinforced by the fact that when she said my name, I told her to stop. Because she'd said my name in a breathy and needy voice, after tearing open my shirt, just as impatient and needy as me. And I couldn't handle it. It was too much. Hearing her say my name like that, for the first time, made everything ... vibrate. Everything was already on fire from touching her, anything else was unbearable. So I told her that. I think I told her that. Maybe not in those exact words, but I'd thought I'd gotten the point across.

I hadn't. She'd thought I was drawing the lines of our relationship or putting her in her place or some stupid shit like that. When what I'd really meant was she had such an insatiable effect on me that even little things like that killed me. But I couldn't say that. It didn't sound sane.

And then there were the dinners. Dinners Mother forced upon me, under the impression I was lonely or getting old enough to settle down and have children or whatever other ridiculous idea my mother had. I'd never told her that I had Rachel, that I was far from lonely or in need of anything else. If I had, even without mentioning Rachel by name, Mother would have dug, would have insisted she meet my woman, and eventually drive her away. So I didn't say anything. I let Mother set up these dinners and had Rachel arrange them.

But I had her arrange them so she knew everything, so she had the opportunity to sabotage them if she so chose. She never did, never said anything about them. So I took that to mean that she trusted me, that our relationship was secure, that it was clear that she was the only woman I was interested in. But Rachel didn't see it like that. She didn't care about those women because they weren't a threat to our relationship, but because there was no relationship to threaten.

I punched the steering wheel, accidentally hitting the horn and drawing the attention of those around me. I ignored them and focused on the sting in my hand.

I couldn't understand how Rachel didn't see how badly I needed her. Didn't see that she was the only thing I ever wanted anymore. It should have been obvious. I called for her nearly every damn day, I always found little ways to touch her, hold her. But it wasn't enough. That didn't satisfy her the way it satisfied me. She needed dates. She needed an emotional connection. A connection she thought I'd been unwilling to give, uninterested in. And so she found a man who, at the very least, had the potential to fulfill those needs. Someone she was willing to quit her job for. Quit me for.

No, fuck that. I was going to give her what she needed. That's what I always wanted to do. That's what I'd intended on doing all along. If she'd only said something, I ... I should've asked. I should've used my fucking words two fucking years ago, made it clear I wanted her as mine and mine alone. Made it clear that I was serious about her, whatever the hell that meant. I'd thought it'd been clear, I'd thought she'd understand from ... from the way I looked at her, the way we were drawn together, the way I needed her.

I'm a fucking idiot.

Words. I needed words and a plan. And maybe flowers and chocolates and anything money could buy that she could possibly want.

I had spent the entirety of my evening essentially stalking Rachel's Instagram in the hopes of finding out whatever I could that would make her mine, really mine. And I'd discover two things. One was that she liked sunflowers. There were several photos of her in a field of them, a white sundress blowing in the breeze, a bright smile. She looked happy. I couldn't help but wonder how she'd look if I was the one taking her out to that field or whatever it was. I wouldn't even know how to go about it. Is it just some field you can walk up to? A park? Or was it like apple picking, where you paid an entrance fee? I bet she'd like apple picking.

The second thing I discovered was my limit for seeing her with other men. She posted a good deal; brunch and nights out with friends, weekend outings to museums and parks, and the men who made appearances in the photos made my skin boil. There'd been several photos over the last few months with this one man, Greg. And I knew it was him. The captions were never too specific, she didn't call him her boyfriend or anything, but I knew. And seeing that man, seeing how he looked at her, seeing the kissy faces she made at him, knowing it was his name she was calling out in bed instead of mine, my laptop flew across the room.

The second thing I discovered was my limit for seeing her with other men. She posted a good deal; brunch and nights out with friends, weekend outings to museums and parks, and the men who made appearances in the photos made my skin boil. There'd been several photos over the last few months with this one man, Greg. And I knew it was him. The captions were never too specific, she didn't call him her boyfriend or anything, but I knew. And seeing that man, seeing how he looked at her, seeing the kissy faces she made at him, knowing it was his name she was calling out in bed instead of mine, my laptop flew across the room.

I stood, awkwardly, just outside the elevator, taking her in. She was wearing a loose sweater dress today. Something I hadn't seen her in before.

It hid her body behind scratchy fabric and covered all the bits I loved, *needed*, to touch. And she'd done it because of me, so as not to tempt me.

It burned. One, that she felt the need to do that, like I was some animal that would pounce when I saw skin. Two, it wasn't even effective. There was nothing she could do that would make me not want to touch her, hold her. I just as badly wanted to tangle those short curls around my finger, have those brown eyes on me, as I wanted her bare skin pressed against mine.

Shit. Just a glance and I was already desperate for her. And I'd told myself not to be too eager. I might only have two weeks, which was my own damn fault, but rushing her would probably make things just as bad.

"Good morning, sir." Rachel hadn't looked up to speak, which meant she'd sensed me standing there, watching her, acting like the driveling mess of a man I was trying to pretend I wasn't. So much for not looking eager.

I swallowed back my nerves and strode to her desk. She didn't look as I approached and instead stayed focused on whatever she was working on. So when I stopped in front of her, I set the flowers on her keyboard, forcing her to stop. She paused, fingers hesitantly tracing the lines of the petals before looking up at me. She sucked her lips in, brow furrowing and smoothing like she was trying to hide her reaction.

God, I could barely breathe when she was looking at me, how the hell was I supposed to talk to her about my emotions?

"What are these for, sir?"

I grunted, already frustrated with myself for letting her call me sir or Mr. Bleckard for so long. I raised my eyebrow, trying to play it cool, trying to look like my heart wasn't hammering in my ears right now. "I'd like to take you out on a date this evening. It's customary to bring a woman flowers when you're asking her out, right?"

"You're serious?"

"Yes. I said as much yesterday, didn't I?" Or was that another thing I assumed got across without spoken words?

I mean, yeah. But I kinda thought you'd regret saying that by the morning. Like you'd wake up and realize I wasn't worth the trouble, that you can just get the same thing from your next secretary. It'd definitely be easy to hire someone else if you put that in the ad description."

"I'm not in the habit of fucking my secretaries, Rachel," I said, but I couldn't bring myself to say the more important thing. That she is worth the trouble, that she's worth anything. "So let me take you out tonight."

"Mr. Bleckard, I'm not sure that —"

"Morgan. Call me Morgan. Please." Hearing her use my last name was like torture now that I knew it'd made her feel unimportant.

"Mr. Bleckard, I'm not sure that —" "Morgan. Call me Morgan. Please." Hearing her use my last name was like torture now that I knew it'd made her feel unimportant.

"Have you talked to him yet? Told him you wanted things to get serious?" Ice ran through my veins at the thought, dulling any excitement of hearing her say my name. She didn't take what I'd said yesterday seriously, so she might've already written me off, made the decision that would gut me.

"... no. I was going to talk to him tonight. We have plans for dinner." Rachel bit her bottom lip, letting her gaze drop to the floor. Relief and anxiety twisted in my gut. I had a chance, barely, to convince her to not do that.

"Then let's go out for lunch, so I can show you why that's not something you want to do. Show you that I can make up for whatever's been missing." I leaned across her desk so that I could whisper in her ear and keep her from seeing my face. "Please, Rachel. I'm serious about this."

"But ... you have a meeting during lunch." Her words were soft this time, losing the argumentative tone she had just seconds ago. Surely that was a good sign.

"Reschedule it for tomorrow, please. I'll make the reservations and forward them to you." I held my breath, waiting for her to acknowledge my request. When she finally nodded, I pulled away to look at her. She was hesitant, still biting her lip, but she didn't look like she was about to take it back. So I accepted it as good as I was going to get for now and walked to my door.

I looked at the doorknob, taking a deep breath before adding, "And for what it's worth, I'm sorry. For the misunderstanding. I should've clarified what I wanted, what I'd been expecting. I don't blame you for my failings. This is my fault."

Shit. I should've looked at her as I apologized. *God damn it, Morgan, pull it together. You've never been so lost over a woman.*

And really, wasn't that the whole point?

Chapter Five

Rachel

What do you do when you're in shock because I'm pretty sure that's what's happening. Do you hallucinate things when you're in shock? There's no way Bleckard had been serious about convincing me to really date him. Right?

But the ding of my phone, which only made a sound for Bleckard, told me that everything that just happened was in fact for real. And I simply didn't know how to process it.

Bleckard wanted a real relationship. An exclusive one, if I was picking up on the right cues this time. The man who was a rich playboy with a dash of commitment-phobia vibes wanted me to be more than just some fuck buddy. It felt like this was coming out of nowhere. Like he was only acting like this because I threatened his status quo. And sure, I wasn't in love with Greg yet, but like hell was I going to start a relationship just because this man wanted to keep fucking me. Because that was it, right? That was the only logical answer for all of this.

I looked over my shoulder at Bleckard's door, as if it would give me some clue as to what the man inside was thinking. And while I was staring, Bleckard stepped out. He looked me in the eye, his gaze holding mine, and ran his fingers through dark blond waves before letting out a long breath.

"Did you get the reservation?"

"Yes, sir." His brow furrowed. "Yes, Morgan."

His name felt weird on my lips. Not in a bad way, just … unfamiliar. But the way his facial muscles relaxed when he heard me say it made my heart … do something. It's not like he smiled, the man didn't smile, just smirk when he knew he was doing something incredible to my body. But this reaction was more than I'd ever gotten outside of sex. He really was very expressive during sex. I wonder why that was. Did he think that was the only time he could speak like that?

"Good. I'll be busy until then, so don't disturb me unless it's an emergency." And then he was gone. The curtness didn't bother me, but it did bring his earlier words into contrast. It wasn't like he'd been begging me for a date. But …

No, no, no. I was overthinking this. Bleckard didn't really want a serious relationship. He barely wanted to do anything outside of work. I'd just point this out at lunch and he'd realize that we wouldn't work out together, not for the type of relationship I was pursuing.

Then my hands fell back to the flowers. Sunflowers weren't exactly in season, so it must have taken him a good amount of time to find them. Effort. That's what the flowers said to me. He was putting in the effort to convince me that he was serious.

I shook my head, trying to get rid of the thoughts bogging me down. Then I got up to grab a vase for the flowers. And, since I knew Bleckard wouldn't mind, I spent a few minutes arranging them just right so I could take a picture. I captioned it as "A little something to brighten my day". Looking at it in the feed, I saw it as a post about a woman bragging about her man, who bought her flowers just because. I liked the idea of it, of being dotted on like that. Was that something Bleckard wanted to do? Or was this just a once-off to convince me to be his?

Fuck thinking. I had work to do.

I shook my head, trying to get rid of the thoughts bogging me down. Then I got up to grab a vase for the flowers. And, since I knew Bleckard wouldn't mind, I spent a few minutes arranging them just right so I could take a picture. I captioned it as "A little something to brighten my day". Looking at it in the feed, I saw it as a post about a woman bragging about her man, who bought her flowers just because. I liked the idea of it, of being dotted on like that. Was that something Bleckard wanted to do? Or was this just a once-off to convince me to be his? Fuck thinking. I had work to do.

Whatever. If this was how he wanted it to be, it was just more proof that our idea of a serious relationship didn't match up. This behavior proved my point. It unfortunately also proved that Bleckard wasn't as serious as he sounded this morning. Which admittedly wounded my pride a little. It's not like I wanted him, but he said he wanted me and I believed him.

"Your table is ready, Mr. Bleckard." The hostess guided us through the restaurant, passing by several of Bleckard's business acquaintances. They all nodded to us and while I returned the gesture, Bleckard didn't. Which was odd. Bleckard was far from social, but he normally managed a quick nod without prompting. Whatever he was looking at must be important.

Nope, none of my business. I didn't care about his phone or whatever was on it.

"So, do you ... do you have a nickname?" Bleckard asked once we were seated and the hostess had walked away. His phone dipped in his hand as he looked up at me, but his thumb was still poised over the screen.

"What?" It was the only thing I could say, because where the hell had that question come from? Bleckard's shoulders tensed and he looked back at his phone for a beat before returning his gaze to me.

"Do you have a nickname? Or any other name you go by?"

"Um ... I — not really. My brother's kids call me Ray, but that's really only because they can't say Rachel yet. They're only one, so their vocabulary is limited. I wouldn't want another adult to call me that though."

My answer came out a little frazzled, still dumbstruck by the odd question. Bleckard on the other hand nodded before his thumb moved over his phone.

"And your family, what are they like?"

What the hell kind of questions are these? Was this some sort of shitty first-date interview? Did he really think a round of basic, impersonal questions was going to solve anything between us?

"Mr. Bleckard, why — what's with these questions?"

He looked down at his phone again, biting his lip. "You said we didn't know each other. I'm trying to correct that."

Oh, I didn't think I'd actually be right.

"Okay, but these questions are a little one side, don't you think?"

"You already know everything about me, Rachel." Bleckard's jaw twitched, the way it did when I hadn't picked up on his hints or when someone questioned him on something about his business. I read that look as irritation. Was he irritated that I was questioning how to go about this second chance? Not that this relationship was a thing to begin with, but still.

"I know your coffee order. If that's enough to know you as a person, then I'm not sure you're the kind of man I want to date. And to be clear, when I say that, I mean I'm looking for something long-term, someone to settle down with. Someone who'll go out with me to do shit, like concerts or shows or whatever. Someone who'll spend rainy days cuddling on the couch with me and binging dumb reality shows. Someone who'll take a hundred pictures of me in front of some tourist shit until we get the perfect one. Is that really what you want? Something more than sex and convenience?"

"Yes." His response was automatic. And his jaw twitched like he was trying to work out more words. Eventually, he looked away and said, "I'm aware I'm not an interesting man. I would hope I make up for it in other ways, but I understand that even in that regard I've not ... measured up. I want you though. In whatever form that takes. I'll take you wherever you want, to do whatever you want. All you have to do is ask."

"Would you go get your nails done with me?" I don't really know why *that* was what I asked about. It's not like I'd ever gotten previous partners to do it. Maybe I was just deflecting his answer with a joke.

Bleckard looked back at me, eyes narrowed like he was trying to figure out if I was joking or not. I tried to keep a straight face, partly because I didn't even know if I was joking. But whatever his answer was, it would determine how I'd feel for the rest of the meal. Bleckard looked down, flipping his hand that held his phone and examining his nails.

"Clear polish is a thing, yes?" When I nodded, he copied the gesture and sighed. "I'm not exactly sure what getting our nails done entails, but if it'll make you happy, I'll do it."

That was a really good answer. An answer that I'm not sure I wanted to hear. So instead of taking that to heart, I continued with the joke, upping the ante.

"So if I asked for your credit card, you'd ..." I trailed off, giving him a bright smile, the kind of smile that I thought would make it clear that I was just teasing him. But when he just raised an eyebrow and fished out his wallet, my smile faltered to hold back a laugh. And when he set the black card down between us, I broke. To his credit, he didn't say anything. He simply withdrew his hand, crossed his arms, and leveled me with a narrow look.

"I'm sorry, Morgan, I was just joking. I didn't think you'd actually give me your card." I spoke through giggles, the fit getting worse as I watched Morgan's face ease, the corner of his lip tilting up. It wasn't quite a smile, but it had a similar effect.

"Take it anyways. As an apology. I'm sure there have been a few expenses you've accrued because of me."

"You mean the clothes you've torn? Or the waxes?" I teased, suddenly finding it hard to stop smiling.

"Were the waxes for me?"

"Yes." I could feel my cheeks start to burn, but I didn't look away. I was curious to see how he'd react. I didn't start getting waxed for Morgan. I'd gotten in the habit of waxing for the summer back in college. But he'd been … appreciative the first time he'd had me after a wax. And that sort of appreciation was addictive. And if the admission that Morgan was part of the reason I kept up that particular routine with that particular grooming habit on a more regular basis meant anything, well, so what?

"Did you think it was necessary?" Morgan chewed at his bottom lip.

"No." Given how Morgan felt about period sex, I'm pretty sure there was nothing that would keep him from fucking me.

"Good. But, even if by coincidence, I'm the one enjoying those sorts of things, I should be the one paying for it. Use the card. For your waxes, your nails, your clothes, whatever makes you happy."

"You really mean that?"

"Have I ever given the impression that I say things I don't mean?"

"No, sir. In fact, I probably take you a little too literally because of that." I let out a breathy laugh before shaking my head. I was starting to warm up to the idea of treating this date like … well a date. And that thought was really overwhelming and I wasn't really ready to think about it. So I pushed it aside. I could examine the results of this date and how they affected my feelings afterward. There was no harm in just letting this moment be.

"Anyways, back to your questions. I'm assuming you don't have a nickname, right?"

"Correct."

For some reason, the short answer pulled a smile out of me. It was just so … Morgan.

"All right, then family, right?" Morgan nodded. "My family is ... all right, I guess. I'm not super close with my parents, though my mom tries but in a forceful, here's what you should do with your life and if you don't do it I'll take offense type of way. And that can get really ... tiring. I guess we sorta have that in common." Morgan let out a breath, something between a sigh and a laugh. "Yeah, you'll have to talk about that next. But I have two brothers, one older and one younger. We've always gotten along pretty well. I mean after the whole teenage, my sister's the most annoying person on the planet phase. My younger brother is a total manwhore though. Conveniently he's never pulled aside and given a talking to about settling down like me, but that's the double standard for you. My older brother is the total opposite. He met his wife in high school and was done from day one. They live out in Brexton with their kids. I go out to visit them a lot, mostly because my sister-in-law is one of my best friends. Their kids are real cute too, so that doesn't hurt. Always have sticky hands though. Can't ever go over without a change of clothes."

Morgan nodded, pulling his phone back out and typing something. What was that about?

"Do you want ... them?" He choked a little on the words before clearing his throat.

"Want what?" I leaned forward, trying to make it look like I was looking at the menu when I really wanted a glimpse of his phone. Was he reading off a list of first-date questions? And then making notes? That would be kind of cute. But Morgan flipped his phone down on the table, eyes wide for a moment before his features returned to their usual cool and unreadable demeanor.

"Children."

"Oh." I settled back in my chair and tried to clear my throat. This was the bit that always held me back when I tried to find someone "serious". It was why I'd given up looking for someone long before I met Morgan. "No,

I don't. I'm not particularly interested in the aftereffects of childbirth on my body. My mom had a lot of health issues after me and they got worse after my brother. So it's a big no for me."

Morgan opened his mouth to reply, but whatever he was going to say was cut off by the waiter finally coming to take our drink orders. With that done, we were left in an awkward silence. A silence that lasted until our drinks were brought out. And while I was used to Morgan's quiet spells, this one didn't feel natural. So I downed my drink and bit the bullet.

"So what about you? Do you want kids?"

Bleckard looked up from his drink taking a sharp breath. "I would never want something that would hurt you or put your health at risk."

God, it was a good thing I'd already swallowed my drink.

"Um, I — that's — is that your actual answer or just your answer for me?" While I stood firm on my no kids position, I also was firm on not changing anyone's mind either. Wanting kids wasn't something you just gave up on because of somebody else. That type of desire didn't go away. And if Bleckard was just saying that because he wanted me more than he wanted a kid right now, then ... I don't know. I'd have to walk away, I guess.

"I'll admit, I never gave it much thought. I'm sure my mother would want a grandchild, so any desire I've ever had for a kid was more so out of the desire to please her than anything else. But you've had to sit in on my calls with her, I'm not sure she'd be pleased with anything. So no, I don't want a child." Morgan spoke looking away from me, which he'd been doing a lot during this conversation. And he normally wasn't the type of man to look away. And he certainly wasn't the type of man who'd open up about his feelings like that. And I wanted to hear more. I was hungry for it.

"You feel a lot of obligation to your Mother, huh? Is that why you take her calls even though they clearly annoy you?"

Morgan shifted, still looking away from me, and crossed his arms, fingers tapping an uneven rhythm.

"Yes. She's my mother after all. I wouldn't say her calls annoy me ... but they come close. She's the one who gave me money to start this business, money for college. And I think deep down, she wants to see me happy, she just has a different definition of what would make me happy."

"And your father?" I asked, resisting the urge to ask what would make him happy. Because even after two years, I had no fucking clue. I knew what made him content and comfortable, the burritos from St. Luca's, hazelnut coffee from Diana's, and Kenny G at volume 18. But that stuff doesn't make him smile, ergo they didn't make him happy. And right now, I kinda wanted to see that smile.

"I don't know who he is. Mother was never particularly inclined to talk about him. So, no siblings either, if you were wondering."

"That you know of."

Morgan turned to look at me, eyes narrowed. And oops, that joke definitely shouldn't have come out of my mouth. Even though Morgan was opening up to me, we weren't exactly make jokes about your absent father close. And come to think of it, his father could just as easily have passed when he was born.

"Rachel?" he said, an eyebrow raised as he stared down at me.

"Yes, sir?" The corner of his lip twitched. Right. He wanted me to call him by name. But I definitely couldn't do that when I'd just risked pissing him off. If he was mad, what would that mean for us, for my job?

"Did you just make a joke about my absent father?"

I nodded and jumped when he laughed. Not a polite smirking sound, but an actual deep-down chuckle. And the sound was just as warm as it was surprising.

Chapter Six

Morgan

I spend very little time thinking about my father. In fact, the only time I'd thought of him in recent memory was when my doctor asked about my family history. So I was far from offended by Rachel's off-handed comment. In fact, it solidified that she was perfect for me. Just because I was a serious person, people seemed to think they had to be serious as well. Rachel making a joke like that made me feel like ... I wasn't being left out.

And the way her breath caught when she thought I'd be mad, the way she switched back to saying sir? I can't deny the effect it had on my cock. Maybe that was the reason I'd never brought myself to have her call me by name. I wasn't emotionally ready and the sir thing was hot as fuck. If sir was the only thing she'd call me in bed, I'd take it. That is if I could get her in my bed at all. My bed. Not my office or some hotel room, my actual bed. If I get to fuck her again, it'll be there.

I shook my head, trying to push away the sexual thoughts. If I let my mind wander any further, my body would be ready faster than I could think against it. I needed to focus on the plan.

I tapped my phone a few times to bring up the list of 52 things Google said I needed to know about Rachel to have a successful relationship. I'd copied the article into my notes app and made notes as we talked. I wasn't going to risk forgetting a single thing she was willing to share with me. But 52 was too much to go over one lunch and there was only so much time we'd have over the next two weeks.

"I really am sorry, though," Rachel murmured, a small blush creeping up her cheeks. And, without much thought, I took her hand that had been fisting in her napkin on the table. I unraveled her grip and entwined our fingers. I'd always thought holding hands was an unnecessary action, but it felt right in this moment, natural. And the way her blush spread faster across her cheeks changed my mind indefinitely. Suddenly I was wondering how we could rearrange my office so we could sit side by side, holding hands all day.

"I'm not offended, Rachel." I don't think there's a single thing she could do that would offend me. Kill me on the inside, sure. But not offend me. Those words should be easy to say, they were right there, fully formulated and ready to go. But something kept them stuck, lodged in my throat.

"So you're okay with jokes like that?" When I nodded, her redness started to fade, the tension in her shoulders eased, and that soft smile returned. "But not about your mom, right?"

I paused for a moment. Then the moment stretched as I tried to imagine the lines of what would and wouldn't upset me regarding my mother. She was a difficult woman to please with a sharp tongue. If she was even mildly put off, you heard about it. She spent my money freely, as if she'd always had it to begin with. It was all, to my understanding, a front. Having a child out of wedlock meant my grandparents' disownment. And now that I had the money to give her whatever life she chose, she picked up where she imagined her life should have gone.

There was plenty to poke fun at and she'd deserved it in most cases. But there was a line somewhere and I didn't know where it was.

"You can just say no, Morgan. It's not like I have to make jokes about your mom. And certainly not to you." That comment pulled at the corner of my lips.

"It's not a no."

Rachel tilted her head, waiting for me to add more. But I still didn't have an exact answer.

"I never would've guessed you were such a momma's boy." There it was again, that teasing smile. I don't know how a smile communicated that she was joking, but it did. Something about the unevenness of it. Or maybe the way the corners of her eyes wrinkled.

"I don't think I am." Should I be teasing her back? How did that work? What would I say and how would I make it certain she knew I was joking?

"I mean, you definitely don't look it. Your mom doesn't seem especially affectionate either. But she's still the most important person in your life, right?"

My brow furrowed. She was technically right, but also …

My grip on Rachel's hand tightened and she squeezed back, her thumb gently stroking mine. "I'm not a super big fan of people asking me what I'm feeling in the moment. Sometimes it takes me a hot minute, or hour, to process anything. My mom calls it avoiding the problem. A big point of tension in my household, especially since I can be super impulsive in other ways. But we can skip that question and go to the next one."

She nodded to my phone in front of me, its screen already black. It seemed like an important fact, that Rachel didn't process her feelings immediately. So I filed that away as I revived my screen to show the next question.

"Do you have a weird habit?"

"Huh. You know, that's one of those questions where, as soon as it's asked, I can't think of a single thing." Rachel chewed at her bottom lip, head tilting to the side as she thought.

"Your candy wrappers."

"What?"

"Whenever you have a piece of candy, or gum or anything else with a wrapper, you fold it. First into a square, then in triangles." Her mouth dropped before she let out a breathy laugh.

"Yeah, I guess that's pretty weird, huh? I didn't think anyone ever noticed."

"I bet Greg hasn't." The words were out of my mouth before I could think better of them. I was just so desperate to prove I knew her better. Thankfully, Rachel didn't seem bothered by the comment. She shrugged and looked away, off into the distance.

"I mean, we haven't known each other that long," she murmured. And then her brow furrowed and she added, "Wait, I never said his name."

Fuck. I really shouldn't have said anything. What would she think if I admitted to scrolling through her Instagram all night? Would she think I was a pathetic creep?

"Whatever. What's your weird thing? And it can't be how you're anal about your working environment. That's, like, a thing for every CEO." Did she just call me anal? How had I gone two years without this side of her personality? I'd been so wrong thinking that our bodies communicated everything, that my need for her said it all. If this was just a glimpse at what Rachel was like, really like, when she wasn't treating me like a boss or a ... fuck buddy, then I'd been missing out on so much. So much of her. I was such an idiot.

"I ..." My mouth opened to give her an answer, but nothing came readily. The only things I could think of were too revealing, showed just how much I felt for her, showed just how horribly mistaken I'd been about our relationship. Things like how the only picture on my bedside table was one of her, so her face was the first thing I saw in the morning and the last thing I saw at night. That one time, during her first week working for me, she'd accidentally played her music without the headphones plugged in all the way and I listened to that song on repeat for a week. That I kept a closet's worth of clothes for her in the office, in case I was an impatient asshole and ruined her clothes again or if she spilled coffee or something. But I couldn't say any of those things out loud.

"You're right, it's hard to think of something like that off the top of your head."

"Did you forget that you spend exactly 43 minutes in the gym every Tuesday and Thursday evening? That's pretty odd if you ask me."

"It's the length of my playlist."

"What's on the playlist?"

The first ten songs I heard her play or sing.

"Just ... some songs. But I also go on Saturdays." I grit my teeth, remembering just how boring my routines were in comparison to how she went out and actually did things every weekend. I tapped my phone back to life, typed the answer, and scrolled to the next question. I'd confirmed that the list had been made by doctors or counselors, but maybe I should've searched for something more effective. The time limit, something I'd set, weighed on me, made me feel rushed to do things I simply hadn't thought to do before but should have done, since day one. "What were you like in high school?"

"Is this your list of questions for all your dates?" Rachel asked, nose scrunching up in a way that would've warmed my heart if not for the implication that what I was doing here, asking all these things, wasn't important, specific to her.

"I don't go on dates."

"So what happened with those other women? I mean, I know you never had me arrange any other dinners and for the most part, none of them called the office asking for you." Rachel started to pull her hand away from mine, but I didn't let go. When she looked up to meet my gaze, something there stopped her from pulling away. God, I hope it wasn't the desperation she saw.

"For the most part, the women talked and I nodded. But none of them changed the fact that you're the only woman I've been interested in." You're the only woman I need. God, I thought I'd been disgustingly obvious before. Just saying those few words felt like I was screaming my need for her. Would this feeling ever ebb? This sensation that I was ripping out a piece of myself and handing it over to her. Why did it feel like that?

"Um ... just for the sake of ... open communication, I guess. Greg isn't the first man I dated. I thought since we didn't ever talk about things or go out or anything, that we weren't a committed thing. So I've been ... dating around. And ..." She trailed off, looking away again. But I needed her eyes on me, needed her to see the things I had trouble putting into words.

I tapped my thumb on her and her eyes came back to mine. "I understand. It's not your fault I made a different assumption."

It was all I could manage to get out. It was all my fault. If I wanted her all to myself, and I desperately did, I should've said so. I should've known what I was doing wasn't enough. Should've noticed that there were typical couple milestones we never reached, like meeting the parents, going to each other's place, and celebrating an anniversary. I'd assumed that we didn't need those milestones, that just because we didn't do them, didn't mean our relationship was lacking.

Rachel sucked in a deep breath, mouth opening to say something, then shook her head. "Well, I was that typical awkward girl in high school. You know, quiet, kept to herself, super shy. College is where I really came out of my shell. Mostly 'cause my mom wasn't around to judge my every move. But what about you? Were you super serious in high school too?"

"I ... I played tennis," I offered up because I didn't want to admit that, while not as serious, I was just as stoic and curt as I am now. That attitude was fine as a grown man who didn't need anything from anyone. But as a teenager? Shit, I probably would've wanted to punch me.

"Tennis?" Rachel repeated.

"My mother wanted me to play a sport. It was a sort of malicious compliance. I picked something I thought she wouldn't be interested in watching, something less likely to get a scholarship somewhere that didn't have the classes I wanted."

"Tennis seems right up your mom's alley, though. She's got major country club vibes."

"We didn't exactly have country club money back then, but yeah, I'm pretty sure that's what she was picturing when I signed up."

"And were you any good?"

"No, absolute rubbish. Couldn't hit the ball to save my life."

"Oh man, is it bad that I wanna see you play just because of that?" She was laughing at me now, a quiet laugh that she covered with a hand. How had I not realized how much warmth her laughter could bring me? How had I ever been satisfied before with just sex? This simple date, this conversation, it brought a deeper, different satisfaction. Something that warmed me to my bones.

I held back a smile and looked down at my phone, frowning at the next question. Love languages. What the fuck was that?

"Run out of date questions … sir?" My gaze flicked up to see Rachel's mischievous smile. The smile that I had always taken to mean that she wanted me. But maybe it really meant that she was daring me to resist her. And I'd lose that dare every day of the week, every minute of the day, every single second of my life.

"No. What's your love language?" Maybe if I said it confidently enough, she wouldn't figure out I had no idea what that meant. And I would have Googled it, but I couldn't tear my eyes away from her reaction. That mischievous smile faded into confusion, her brow furrowing and she bit her lip as she thought.

"Um, I don't really know what it falls under, but … when somebody proves they've been listening, even to the shit I ramble on about. Like, if I made a comment about how I was excited for the new Starbucks drink and they get it for me. Or if I complain about something, like losing my keys, and they get me a key hook by the door or something. Or if they notice — you know, things like that."

Something about her answer felt satisfying. I could do that. I might not have said the right words our whole relationship, but I've paid attention. I just needed to take action on all the little things I'd thought of doing that seemed like they'd be too much, be inappropriate, or nuisances. Like the drink she mentioned. There'd been a time when she was excited for some flavor coming out and I'd gotten as far as buying the damn thing, but when I got to the office, she already had a drink, so I dumped it out.

"Are you two ready to order?" Our waiter asked and instinctively I glared at him for interrupting my moment with Rachel. But then she started to pull away, so I relaxed my features and held her tighter.

"Yes, thank you. I'll have the steak, medium-rare. And …" Before lunch, I would've assumed what she wanted. But my assumptions seemed rotten and I couldn't trust that instinct.

"And I'll have the salmon. Thank you," Rachel said, ordering exactly what I thought she would. We handed our menus over and in the process, she let go of my hand and I instantly missed the warmth. But then she returned it like it was the natural thing to do. And I still didn't understand love languages, but this. This was it.

Chapter Seven

Rachel

"Can I kiss you, Rachel?"

My hands froze halfway through buckling myself in. Morgan sat in the driver's seat, turned towards me, one hand twitching in his lap.

Something about him asking to kiss me after our date made things … feel different. And it scared me.

I'd been serious when I told him I didn't do well processing my emotions in the moment. Whenever I said something in the moment, it always turned out rotten. Like when my high school boyfriend told me he loved me and I said it back because that's what was expected. Except when I realized I wasn't in love with him and told him such, he was so upset he broke up with me. It wasn't exactly a great situation, so I avoided making snap decisions like that ever since.

And right now, it felt like I was on the verge of making another hasty decision. Kissing him in this state would be a bad idea. Because with Morgan, it wouldn't end in a kiss. Especially since it'd been days since we'd last fucked. And he needed that touch, needed the warmth of our bodies.

In retrospect, it should've been obvious that his love language was physical touch.

"I'm not sure that's a good idea," I whispered. My voice caught in my throat, stuck by all the ideas and emotions that needed to be dealt with. It seems I'd misunderstood everything in regard to how Morgan felt about me. He wanted a full relationship, with dates and talking and going out to events and meeting the families. He'd just hadn't known how to express it. And if I said yes to him, that meant I'd have to talk to his mom more, break things off with Greg, introduce him to my brother, and ... No, that wasn't what he was asking for right now. He just wanted a kiss.

"Just a kiss. Please." The way he echoed my thoughts made me nod. Even though I wasn't certain it would be just a kiss. How was I going to resist climbing on his lap? Would he be able to stop his hands from sliding up my dress? Because this date, all the talking and laughing and getting to know each other, satisfied something in me. And with that satisfied, my libido wanted its turn.

"Just a kiss," I repeated, moreso to remind myself of the fact that sex would be a bad idea right now. Even if a part of me didn't understand why I was denying myself.

Morgan leaned in slowly, his eyes never leaving mine. They seemed brighter than usual as he closed the distance. One hand moved up, cupping my cheek, and he rested his forehead against mine. For a long moment, we stayed like that, breathing each other's air, our lips hovering over each other.

I've kissed Morgan so many times, I should know what to expect. His kisses were intoxicating. He didn't do slow, he did hungry and needy. But after lunch, something felt different. Something had shifted. So when his lips finally touched mine, warm and soft, a soft groan escaped from deep in my chest. And when I parted my lips, desperate for more, Morgan pulled away.

"What?" The kiss had been short, too short. And not nearly enough. And it felt ... disappointing. Especially after that lunch, after all that connection and talking. I wanted more.

"Was that ... was that too much?" Morgan's chest was rising and falling in quick waves. But I wanted to see him panting.

"Too much? Morgan, you've stuffed your tie in my mouth while fucking me on business calls. That wasn't even close to enough." Frustration and need were the only emotions I could process right now and they were heavy. I shifted in my seat, turning to Morgan and taking hold of his tie, pulling him closer.

"I'm sorry, that was —" I suppose it was decent of him to apologize for that moment. But I'd been fully consenting to it, so it wasn't necessary. What was necessary was fulfilling my needs, and probably his. So I cut him off.

"Kiss me. For real." I'd pulled until we were inches apart, our breaths mingling again. And then, as soon as the words were out of my mouth, Morgan's lips were in mine, fingers tangling into my hair. Impatient to feel him, all of him, I parted my lips, raking my tongue over his bottom lip. Morgan opened with a sigh, the sound feeding my ego and need. I grazed his tongue, moaning when he tangled his with mine. Everything lit sparks within me, the sensation hotter than the normal goosebumps he inspired.

My hand drifted, letting the tie slip through my fingers as I made my way down. I'd intended to tease him, let my fingers gaze over his belt before resting my hand on his thigh. But his erection distracted me, which it often did. But god, he was impressively hard. There was no need to coax him, or me honestly. And suddenly I regretted my choice of clothes this morning. I'd worn a sweater dress with thick leggings, hoping to dull the usual chemistry between us, thinking I wouldn't want more. Now I just wanted them off. Would he be able to rip the thick fabric to get between my thighs? How much maneuvering would we need to do so I could be on his cock?

"Christ, Rachel. I need to stop." Morgan pulled back and pushed my hand away.

"Oh." It was all I could get out with my blood rushing in my ears. I could feel my body slowly get the hint that we weren't about to get fucked and it wasn't taking the news well. I bit my lip, trying not to pout. Logically, I knew this was a good turn of events. Fucking would complicate things further. But god, everything was buzzing and I wanted, *needed* him right now.

"Rachel?"

"Yes, sir?" I wasn't looking at him, trying to find something interesting outside the window to stare at instead.

"I needed to stop kissing you like that because ..." He trailed off and he was quiet for so long, I couldn't help myself from looking back at him. He looked down at the steering wheel, his grip tight. "You said no more sex."

"No, I didn't." The words were out of my mouth embarrassingly fast. But I'm pretty sure I didn't say we couldn't have sex anymore. I mean, I tried to break things off completely, which is arguably the same thing. But since he wanted me to put off that final step, then I didn't need to not fuck him. Right?

"Rachel," Morgan said, his voice a clear warning not to test him on whatever he was about to say. "You said you were looking for something serious, an emotional connection. Yes?"

"Yes."

"And up until yesterday, you thought that wasn't something I was interested in. That I was only fucking you because you were convenient. Yes?" I nodded because I didn't have words anymore, the moment had stolen them. "You understand now that's not what I want, not how I saw things?"

Again, I nodded instead of saying anything. Morgan uncharacteristically filled the silence I left. "I want to be your boyfriend."

"Boyfriend? I don't think I've had one of those since high school," I joked, words finally coming to me, but not the right ones. Morgan's hand took my chin, making sure I was looking at him.

"You know what I mean. I want to be your partner, the only man you see. I'm not fucking you again until that's the case. Understand?"

Since I couldn't make a deflective joke out of that, I nodded again.

"Are you going to wait the two weeks?"

"Two weeks?" God, I couldn't formulate my own words anymore. Especially with his hand on my chin like that. He normally did that when I'd closed my eyes during sex and he wanted to look at me.

"Two weeks to prove I can give you what you've been missing. Prove I'm serious about you, about us. That we could fall in love. I know you're seeing him tonight and that one lunch won't be enough. I just — please give me some more time. I — I didn't know what I was doing wrong before. It'll take me some time to get it right."

Too many thoughts clouded my head at once. Guilt about how the misunderstanding built between us, guilt that Greg might have the same idea, fear of what a serious relationship actually meant. It boiled over to the point that none of the thoughts sounded real, like TV static.

"Yeah. Two weeks is good."

It was a small reaction, but I saw the breath puff out of Morgan before he let go and drove us back to the office.

Small talk with Greg was like a comfort show. It was soft and pleasant and I didn't have to think too hard. It made the wait to be seated for our weekly dinner pleasant. The restaurant, the same Italian place we went to every Tuesday, was small, cozy, and had the rare charm of familiarity that was lacking in the city. I liked it. I liked that there was a tradition here, that I saw the same families I saw last week.

But ... I felt out of place. All the women, even those without kids, had a motherly vibe to them. They dressed plainly, no time put into their appearance. I'm pretty sure I was the only one with my nails done. And I felt a little judged for it. Not that anyone said anything, but I could tell they thought I didn't belong in the family restaurant.

"So, how was your day, hon?" Greg asked once we were seated. I smiled. I liked how he called me hon. It was sweet and homey. But my day had been … unexpected. And I hadn't had enough time to sort through my feelings about Morgan between work and now. So how did I describe my day to a man I thought I wanted? … no, I still think Greg has more potential for a happy, fulfilling future. Maybe.

"Um, actually, there's something we should clarify," I started, not sure how to phrase what I wanted to ask, but needed to confirm. Greg's head tilted, shaggy waves shifting over his shoulders.

"This have something to do with those flowers?" There was a coy smile on his lips, but the tease stung. Maybe I shouldn't have posted a picture of them. Did that make it seem like I was rubbing it in his face that another man bought me flowers? Even if I didn't say anything about Morgan, it'd be easy to jump to that conclusion.

"Yes. I … um, well I just wanted to see if we're on the same page when it comes to …" Ugh, why was this so hard?

"Exclusivity?" Greg offered up. When I nodded, he laughed softly and continued, "Well we've been going out for a while and it's something I'm looking for, in general. So I'd like to work towards that, with you."

I let out a long sigh and Greg laughed again. He laughed a lot. It was a nice, comforting sound. Morgan's laugh was rare, so rare that when I finally heard it, it felt magical. But that didn't mean it was better.

"Good, I'm glad that we're on the same page," I said. Greg, still smiling because he didn't hold that back either, took my hand. The hold was warm. But it didn't have that … something more feel that Morgan had. But maybe I was just doubting everything after what Morgan said.

"That guy wasn't on the same page, huh?" Greg raised an eyebrow as my face began to redden. No way was I going to tell Greg I'd been having a sexual relationship with my boss for two years and I was just now figuring out it meant different things to us. I'm not even sure what I would think if I was in his shoes.

"Not exactly. But that misunderstandings cleared up." Short and sweet. That's all I needed to say. Except … "How do you feel about kids?"

"I mean, I'm a teacher." Greg laughed again and suddenly the sound came off as more grating than comforting this time.

"I know, but I feel like that could go both ways, you know? Either you love kids and can't get enough of them or you deal with kids all day and don't want another one at home to deal with."

"Oh yeah, I guess I could see that. But yeah, I do want kids. You too, right?"

Ah, there it is. I shouldn't have asked. It ruined everything right away. Why did I feel that way, though? I wanted something serious, something that would be death do us part. If it wasn't Greg or Morgan, that didn't matter. Plenty of fish in the sea and whatnot. Just because I'd made up my mind to stop things with Morgan before, didn't mean I'd put all my hopes with Greg.

Except Morgan matched up in this regard.

"No, I don't want kids." I didn't know what to expect. Maybe Greg would get up, explain that's the dealbreaker for him, and leave. Or worse, he'd just laugh it off.

"Oh, don't worry, you'll change your mind, hon."

Oh, that's way worse than laughter. *So much worse.*

But then he dropped the subject and we talked through dinner about his work day, mine, our plans for the rest of the week, and the weekend. And I could almost forget that pivotal difference between us. Almost.

"So …" Greg started as we stepped out of the restaurant. While trying to put on my jacket, I got caught in the sleeve, the fabric twisting so I couldn't slide in. Greg smiled, a small chuckle escaping him. He stepped close to me, fixing my sleeve and pulling the jacket the rest of the way on, his hands resting on my hips. He pulled me in closer, his breath tickling my neck. It didn't send goosebumps down my arms, but it was warm. Could I forget about the kid thing, for just a moment? "What steps do I need to take to make this an exclusive thing?"

"Memorize my body." I hadn't meant to say it, especially like that. But wasn't that the main pull to Morgan? If sex was off the table with him, did I even want to consider him as a boyfriend, as something more? And once I got to know Greg better, especially in bed, things could still work out. We could talk through the kid thing. Maybe compromise on adoption.

"Happily," Greg said, stepping away from me to hail a cab. And without him by my side, I didn't miss the warmth, didn't feel the same excitement to get in bed. But at least I didn't feel emotionally overwhelmed like I did after lunch.

Chapter Eight

Rachel

One year ago

"And Kristoff's report reflects the same thing in his district. None of the managers included a breakdown of the sales though, so I sent reminders for that. And Stella wants your approval on the holiday party budget by Friday. She mentioned something about running the color palette by you too, but I reminded her all party planning details are her responsibility. And then –"

"Rachel."

I looked up from my phone, not surprised but still shaken by the way Bleckard eyed me. Not surprised, but very into whatever he had in mind.

Except we didn't have much time. He had a date set to arrive in 20 minutes. Which did beg the question, why the hell did he want to fuck me when he had a date tonight with some hot heiress his mother already approved of?

I bit my lip and tried to shake off that line of thought. It wasn't my business. We were two consenting adults. That woman was someone he hadn't met. There wasn't any moral ambiguity I needed to feel guilty about. Maybe he just wanted to go a round so he could last longer with Miss Heiress later. Though I knew from experience he had no problem with lasting.

"I don't need any more business updates."

"What do you need?" I kinda hated how fast he got to me. I mean, one look and my voice was already breathy.

Bleckard stood from his desk and took one step towards me. I closed the distance, eager. His hand came up, gliding over my arm, up and up until he cupped my cheek, tilting my head to look into his eyes.

"The same thing you do."

"God, yes." I really didn't understand how Bleckard was such a talker in bed. It made no sense, but god did it get me going.

Morgan's lips crashed to mine, hands moving to my clothes, pulling, tugging. I copied his action, fumbling with his belt buckle, then the zipper. Once we were disheveled enough, Bleckard picked me up, wrapping my legs around his waist and taking two long strides to the closed door. He pinned me there, letting his hands go back to pushing my skirt up and pulling my panties aside. One hand stroked my pussy, long, slow strokes that made me shiver. I reached between us, ignoring the awkward angle, and gripped his hardening cock. He thickened under my touch, grunting nonsense into my neck.

"Harder," he groaned as he slid two fingers inside me, immediately pushing on the spot he knew would make me scream for him. I whimpered, not able to help it, and my grip loosened. Bleckard thrust forward, pinning me further into the door and fucking himself in my hand. Taking the hint, I refocused and tightened my grip, twisting to match his thrusts.

Bleckard's fingers inside me started thrusting in time with his cock in my hand and my head rolled back. I was so close, but I needed him inside me, needed to feel his chest pressed against mine, just needed. And god damn it, Bleckard was the only one who ever really fulfilled that need. "Sir, I need —"

Bleckard pulled his hand out of me and jerked me further up the door, lined up to his dick. My hands went to his shoulders, fingers tightening into the fabric of his dress shirt. It was one of the ones I'd bought him when his luggage was lost on our way to a conference. He wore it a lot now. I wonder if …

"Fuck," I breathed as the head of Bleckard's cock began to work its way inside me. As mentally excited as I was, my body hadn't had a chance to catch up. And it probably didn't help that I hadn't gotten a chance to wet his dick. But Bleckard didn't seem to mind the delay. He rocked, just the tip at first, always pulling back when there was any friction. The slow rhythm was just as tantalizing as it was torturing.

"Morgan, are you in there?" The woman's voice was exactly the kind of voice you'd expect from an heiress, high and sharp. It made me wince, which in turn made me feel bad for judging a woman I didn't know. But then Bleckard tugged the front of my shirt down, pushed aside my bra, and sucked my nipple. Hard. He swirled his tongue over me before letting his teeth graze over the sensitive skin. I covered my mouth, barely muffling my whimpers. The room might be soundproof, but if she was right outside the door, she'd definitely hear us.

Bleckard pulled back and yanked his tie off, the silk sliding around his neck. He balled up the fabric and held it up to my mouth. Normally I wouldn't hesitate, but we were right against the door and that woman was waiting for him. It all felt a little too close to wrong.

"What about …" I couldn't remember the woman's name. I tended to forget any information about the women Bleckard went out with. And I didn't want to think about why I did that.

"Why would I give a damn what she thinks?" he grumbled, still rocking into me. He was maybe halfway in now and I wasn't too proud to admit that the dirty little secret vibes this scenario was giving made it hotter. So I opened my mouth, let him ball his tie there, then buried my face into his neck. Bleckard did the same, pressing open mouth kisses down my neck as he rocked. One of his hands remained on my ass, the other grabbed my breast and squeezed.

"Morgan? You there?" the woman asked, knocking on the door. Bleckard pulled back to look at me, his eyes nothing more than pupils.

"I'm in the middle of something important," he growled out, keeping eye contact with me. And then he slid fully inside me and we both sighed. "There it is."

I heard the woman say something, heard her walk away, but I didn't really process any of it. The only thing I could think of was the pleasure of being filled by this man. Fuck, there was nothing like it. I was gonna get addicted, if I wasn't already.

Chapter Nine

Rachel

Present day

I was a woman with a … healthy sexual appetite. This wasn't exactly news to me. Given how much I'd fuck Morgan throughout the work week only to hook up with whoever over the weekend, I knew I wanted more sex than most people. Or at least more than most of the dudes I've dated.

And I never really cared about it until after I left Greg's place, with a hot ache still sitting uncomfortably in between my thighs. And even after a long session with my vibrator, I still buzzed with need. Pun totally intended.

I squirmed in my office chair, finding it hard to focus on work when Morgan was right there, so perfectly able to fulfill my needs. I know he said he didn't want to, not until everything was … decided I guess. But one more time wouldn't hurt, right? It's not like I'm gonna ride his dick and forget everything he'd said yesterday. Well … I'd at least remember afterward.

Resituating my clothes, and unbuttoning one more button than usual, I stood and walked to Morgan's office. I raised my hand to knock, then dropped it to fiddle with my skirt. What was I so nervous about? We've had a sexual relationship for two years. Just because I'd never initiated sex with him, doesn't mean I can't do it now. Apparently, I could've done it the whole time, apparently I could've asked for the goddamn moon and he'd give it to me. So if I ask for a quick fuck, surely he'll give that to me too.

So with a deep breath, I bit the bullet and knocked.

"Come in." Morgan's voice sounded strained, but I didn't read into it. I opened the door, stepped in, and closed it behind me. As I walked up to his desk, Morgan's eyes raked over me and something about that look made me think he saw everything. Saw my need, saw my request before I could even put it into words.

"Yes, Rachel?" His Adam's apple bobbed and something about that little sign emboldened me. I didn't say anything as I stepped up to his desk and sat on the corner. His eyes were glued to where my skirt shifted up my thigh. It was the same skirt he'd told me not to wear on Mondays. And I'd foregone the leggings today. Was it cold as hell walking into the office this morning? Yes. Did that look make it worth it? Absolutely.

"I think we should revisit the no-sex thing." The words didn't come out as confident as I'd wanted them to, but as I shifted on his desk to sit in front of him, Morgan's eyes became glued to my legs.

"Why do you say that?" Morgan pushed back slightly, giving me the space to spread my legs comfortably and give him a view I'd know he liked. I'd worn this lacy, purple piece I knew he loved. In fact, everything I wore were things I'd noticed he liked. From my clothes to my perfume. I gravitated to all the things that reminded me of him. It was an instinctive pull that my dissatisfaction wouldn't let me ignore.

"Because if I'm not serious with anyone, then there's no reason." And because I need you. *Come on, Morgan, surely you see that much.*

"You saw him last night, didn't you?" Morgan asked, his hands coming up my thighs, fingers spreading over my skin.

"Yes." I shifted closer, trying to get more of his touch, the touch that sent fire through my veins, goosebumps up my arms.

"And you slept with him?" Morgan's eyes found mine, a dark intensity mixed with lust.

"Yes." Both his hands slid up my thighs, fingers sliding under the hem of my skirt.

"And he didn't satisfy you."

He didn't say it like a question, but the implication felt … too big. So I answered it. "I wasn't dissatisfied, exactly. It's hard to ask for more sometimes."

"But you don't have a problem asking me, huh?" His fingers slid back, but before I could complain, his hand fisted into my skirt, jerking the fabric up just a fraction.

"Please, Morgan," I whimpered. I reached out for his tie, wanting to pull him closer, but one of his hands let go of my skirt to stop me. He pressed the back of my hand to his lips, a soft, gentle kiss.

"You said quick fucks in my office weren't enough. What makes you think this will be different?"

Because now I know you'll take care of me now. But that felt way too intimate to say.

When I was silent for too long, Morgan's hand in my skirt started to let go.

"I just wanted more."

"More fucking?" Morgan's jaw clenched, his hand tightening on my skirt.

"Sort of. More … different types of sex. Like, we're always … hungry for each other. And that's hot as fuck. But also, beds are nice, taking our time is nice, lazy morning sex is nice. Just … different vibes. Does that make sense?" God, what was I saying? I wasn't making any sense and after saying all that out loud, I felt stupid for even trying to initiate anything.

"So you were never dissatisfied with our sex?"

"No. I mean, those few times the janitor interrupted us were pretty frustrating, but otherwise, no."

"And you always came?"

"Yes. And I'd really like to do that again. Now. Please." If I was just a smidge less needy, I'd tease him about that, about how my comment seemed to have wounded his ego. But right now, with his hands on me, I was barely keeping from burning up with anticipation. Morgan's eyes searched mine for a moment before he finally, *finally*, took pity on me.

"Lay down, Rachel. I'll take care of you." Morgan let go of my hand and placed his on my collarbone, gently pushing until I complied. Once I was down, his hand trailed along my body. And even though I could barely feel the touch through my clothes, the path his fingers took burned. But when both his hands were finally back in my skirt, they paused.

"I was trying to give you space," Morgan murmured. I pushed up on his elbows to find his eyes glued to my center. "But then you come in here like this, asking me for things. You're doing this to me on purpose, aren't you?"

Then Morgan jerked my skirt up and the sudden action and cool air made me gasp. He slid closer, an arm going around my waist to lift me up and bunch my skirt there. Then he worked on sliding my panties off, resting me back down when they slid past my ass. As the fabric went down my leg, Morgan followed the trail, his nose gliding down my skin.

"I knew that if I saw you today, I'd be looking for a sign, looking to see how things went," Morgan said as my underwear slid off my ankles. "I didn't want to see you satisfied by another man, didn't want to smell him on you. It's fucking pathetic."

Something about Morgan calling himself pathetic caught my attention. Never, and I mean never, had I thought of him as a pathetic man. Confusing, yes. A little intimidating, at times. But never pathetic. Especially right now when he was admitting to more emotion than he'd ever had. What could be pathetic about that?

"But you know how I feel about these clothes, Rachel. This feels like a sign." Morgan's lips met my ankles, placing one soft kiss before grazing his teeth along the sensitive skin. Then he licked the sting, his mouthing moving up, up, up. And all thoughts of his emotions were gone. What emotions? All I knew right now was that I needed him, even if that was stupid and selfish. Even though I should point out that my needy cunt and the corresponding actions shouldn't be counted as a sign.

Morgan's mouth stopped at my knees and paused there for a long moment. When he finally looked up at me, some of the lust had dulled. Both his hands slid up my thighs, his elbows pushing my legs apart as his eyes fell back down. "You don't have to say it. I know it's not really a sign."

I needed to say something. I didn't like that softness in his voice, that resignation. I didn't want to make him feel that way. I wanted to make him feel …

"Morgan," I whispered, still unsure of what needed to be said.

"Don't worry, dear. I know what you need, I'll take care of you. Just relax." Something about the way he said dear, something he'd never done before, soothed me. So I did as he said. I closed my eyes and leaned back, my head teetering on the edge of his desk.

When Morgan deemed I was fully relaxed, his hands shifted on my thighs, fingers pulling me apart. He leaned in, stopping an inch away and just breathing me in.

"Morgan. Fuck." My fingers sunk into his hair, trying to tug him closer. He didn't move though. He stayed an inch away, thumbs stroking my thighs.

"Did you think of me while you were with him?" One thumb edged closer, stroking the edge of my cunt. I lifted my hips, eager for more of his touch. Instead of answering my plea, the hand that wasn't teasing me pinned my waist down.

"Tell me. Please."

"Yes," I whimpered, a little ashamed of the admission. But there was no room left for that emotion when Morgan's mouth was finally on me. He licked me up, stopping at my clit and tracing tight circles over the already tender flesh. And then he repeated the action. Over and over again until I was shaking. And just when I thought I'd actually cry from the desire for more, just *more*, his fingers finally slipped into me. He curled his fingers, pulsing against that spot only Morgan knew how to hit instantly.

"Morgan, please," I whined. I was burning and close, so goddamn close.

"Please what, Rachel? And ... for now, keep calling me sir. I haven't earned the right to hear you come with my name on your lips. Not yet. And ... I can't lie, hearing you ask for things, begging for me in this office while calling me sir? That makes me hard as fuck."

"Shit," I groaned. That was hot. Thinking that I couldn't say his name had bothered me. I could admit that much now. But this framing, like this was a little game we were playing and I'd get everything else I needed and wanted at a different time, that made it exciting.

"Make me come, sir. Please."

"Yes, dear." And he did, sucking my clit into his mouth, swirling his tongue around it, all while drawing circles and pressing against my g-spot. I didn't so much come apart for him as I exploded. Everything was on fire, I was shaking and panting, unable to pull myself up. Morgan was going to have to fuck me like this. I'm not even sure I'd be able to keep my legs around his waist.

"Good girl," Morgan whispered, pulling me out of my daze. I shifted, tilting to the side to look at him. He took his fingers out of me, sucking them clean before leaning in to kiss my clit. The action sent shivers down my spine and made me eager for more. But there wasn't anymore. All he did was sit back up and stroke my thigh.

"Morgan?" I pushed myself up, arms a little shaky.

"Yes, dear?" He looked up at me with an eyebrow raised. Was this a part of the sir thing? Did he want me to ask for everything?

"I want you to fuck me. Sir."

Morgan smirked. I was nearly dying of want and this man just smirked at me.

"That's not happening today, Rachel." His hands slipped under my thighs and he pulled me off his desk and onto his lap. He shuffled so that I was comfortably seated, his throbbing cock pressed against me. I couldn't help but grind against him. Morgan groaned and gripped my hips, pulling me against him but keeping me still.

"Just because you're going back on your word, doesn't mean I am," he whispered, kissing at the skin right under my ear.

"Why? You're —"

Morgan cut me off by thrusting into me.

"I'm fully aware of what you've done to my body, Rachel."

"Then shouldn't I —" Another sharp thrust. My eyes rolled back as Morgan sucked along my throat.

"Should what? Take care of me like I did for you?"

I nodded and moved away from his lips so I could kiss his neck in turn. There was something about his scent, the soft soap and the sharpness that was Morgan, that drove me wild. I'd thought it was his cologne, but now I was thinking it was all him. He was the source of all my needs. And right now, his scent was mixed with mine and that mixture did something to me.

This time, when I rocked against him, he didn't stop me. Instead, his hands slid under my shirt, pressing me closer.

"Please, Morgan, I need you," I whimpered into his ear before grazing my teeth over the soft skin. Morgan stiffened and pulled me away. Stunned, I didn't fight him as he set me back on my feet and pushed his chair back to stand. He looked down at me, his eyes ... hurt.

"No, you don't. You *need* my cock. And I'm not making the mistake of giving it to you if it's the only bargaining chip I have for ... making us partners." Morgan grumbled the last few words, kneeling before I had a chance to speak. He grabbed my underwear and lifted my foot to work them back on. I complied with his movements, too stunned to do anything else.

Is that what this moment made him feel? Like I was using him for sex? I mean I definitely wanted sex, but I wasn't trying to imply that was all he was good for. I knew Morgan better now, at least a little bit. He was thoughtful, way more than I'd ever given him credit for or appreciated. And he was doing a lot of out of character things, stepping out of his comfort zone, just to make something of this mess of a relationship between us. He was trying and I was ...

"Morgan, I didn't mean to —"

"Dinner?" Morgan interrupted, standing to slide my underwear back in place.

"What?"

"Will you go to dinner with me tonight? I'll get us reservations at someplace nicer this time. Something with a better wine menu. You prefer riesling, yes?" Morgan didn't look up at me as he spoke, instead he focused on fixing my skirt and tucking my shirt back in. The care in which he did these two things made my heart flutter.

Which was stupid, he always helped make me look presentable again.

Except now I knew he wasn't doing it so that we weren't caught. He was doing it because it was a small way he could take care of me.

"Rachel, are you available?"

"Yes." Warning bells were ringing in my head and I really couldn't put my finger on why. Everything Morgan was doing was right. Why did that make my heart rate accelerate in a way that scared me?

"Yes to dinner or your wine preference?" Satisfied with my clothes, Morgan stood, eyes locking with mine.

"Both."

"Good. I'll forward you the details once I've made the reservation." Morgan stepped closer, kissing my cheek before adding, "And have a new suit delivered for me by then, please."

Morgan pulled away and confusion furrowed my brow. Then I looked down and saw it. A patch of my wetness, smeared over his still hard cock. Forget the red warning lights, I was seeing red for a completely different reason now.

"I am so, so sorry! I'll get right on that," I mumbled, embarrassment making my words rushed. I turned to leave but Morgan grabbed my wrist and turned me back toward him.

"Don't you dare think I'm anything other than happy to have the proof that I satisfied you on me."

Chapter Ten

S everal hours later and I could still taste Rachel on my tongue. And fuck if it wasn't the sweetest taste I'd ever had. I'd gone so far as to avoid lunch, avoid drinking, just to make it last longer.

Rachel had already brought me a new suit, but I couldn't bring myself to change. It was the best kind of torture to look down at my lap and see her come, to feel myself ache with need and know that satisfaction was a long ways off. Because I meant what I said. I'll satisfy her however she needs to prove I'm the man who should do it long-term. But until that was settled, until she was mine, until she was falling in love with me, until I knew she wanted me for more than my ability to fuck her well, we weren't going to do it.

But god she was tempting. So wet and needy and acquiescent. If I'd let her, she would've eagerly dropped to her knees for me. Or ridden my cock. Or anything I asked.

I didn't want to ask for anything sexual though. I wanted ... something more now.

The alarm on my phone went off, signaling there were 30 minutes until our reservation.

I took a deep breath and stood to change. Despite the temptation, this morning was a good sign. She was, at the very least, more attracted to me than Greg. The man had her in his bed for the night and hadn't even been able to satisfy her fully. *I* was the one she came to for satisfaction.

It wasn't enough anymore. I had been so caught up in that sort of satisfaction, it was all-encompassing for me, but it hadn't been for her. And I had to fix that.

Changing, I was supposed to be changing. Not dreading the possibility of losing Rachel.

I changed clothes quickly, somewhat excited to be in the suit Rachel picked for me. It was a navy set, the fabric smooth to the touch. And it fit perfectly. I liked more than I could describe how she was able to pick something out for me, something that fit and looked good, without my input. It was a little thing, but it proved she knew me on some level, a level no one else knew.

Could I say the same? Did I know her just as well?

I went over to the closet, which had become so full of clothes I thought would suit Rachel that I stored my own backup clothes in the car, and pulled out a dress. I held it up, anxiety tightening in my chest. Showing her this, or any of the obscene amounts of clothes I'd hidden away for her, risked a reaction I wasn't prepared for. At one point, I'd been convinced she'd like the plum wrap dress. But then why hadn't I shown it to her before? Why did I wait for an excuse that never came?

A knock on the door forced me to push aside the anxiety. I walked to the door, opening it just enough to pull Rachel in before closing it again. The action made her giggle, the sound so light and breathy that I couldn't help but kiss her. I cupped her cheek, leaning into her gasp to take her lips. She tasted sweet, like dark chocolate. She must've been dipping into the stash she kept at her desk.

"Hello ..." I bit my tongue to keep from calling her dear again. Rachel might not have minded it in the heat of the moment, when her need required her to overlook it, but saying it now would be different. She might not like it, it might make her think less of me.

"Hi, Morgan. Are you ready to go?" she asked, a little breathless. I nodded, cleared my throat, then thrust the dress towards her. Hesitantly, she took the dress, holding it out between us, blocking my view of her reaction.

"It's gorgeous. When did you have time to get this?"

I should tell her. Doing things for your partner unasked was a good sign for a relationship, right? This should be something she would like. Why did I doubt that so much?

"When you were out," I murmured, looking away and biting my lip. It wasn't technically a lie, but it was pathetic. More pathetic than buying her things and never actually giving them to her.

Rachel lowered her hands, clutching the dress to her chest. Her brow was furrowed as she looked around the room. And when her eyes settled back on me, I knew she was suspicious.

"I didn't leave the office today though."

I swallowed and nodded to the closet at the back of the room. She narrowed her eyes at me, then made her way to the door. I didn't turn to watch her.

I could identify the emotion burning through me as shame, but I couldn't for the life of me say why. Perhaps because this was proof of what a fool I'd been, how far I'd misinterpreted our relationship.

"Oh, wow, these are beautiful," Rachel whispered. "How long have you been ... saving these?"

I finally turned to see a sort of wonder on her face and relief instantly unknotted my anxiety. She liked them. She wasn't immediately repulsed by whatever the gesture meant.

"For a while. Just in case you needed them." Since that first time I tore off her buttons.

Rachel's fingers trailed over the clothes, stopping to rub the fabric between her fingers. She looked back over at me. And then she closed the closet and walked back to me.

"You're uncomfortable," she said. Not a question, but I shrugged in answer. She was quiet for a moment before nodding. "Well then, I better go change then."

She made a step to the door and I grabbed her wrist impulsively. "Where're you going?"

"To the bathroom to change." She said it like it was obvious, like she couldn't possibly be doing anything else.

"Why can't you change here?"

"Oh, that's ... kinda intimate, don't you think?" Rachel's face went red and it was her turn to be embarrassed and look away. I didn't understand it though. I had her nearly naked in this office hours ago. And she'd been fully disrobed more times than I could count. How could changing her clothes, just her top layers, be more intimate than that?

"I know it's silly." The way she filled in my silence didn't sit well with me, so I let go of her and stepped aside.

"It's not silly. I want you to do whatever makes you most comfortable. But ..." I stepped back up to whisper in her ear, "I want your intimate moments. Even if it's just something ... silly, like changing clothes."

I pulled away and watched Rachel think this over. She sucked on her bottom lip before nodding. I just barely held in my sigh of relief. I don't know why I wanted to be here while she changed so badly. Maybe just because she labeled it as an intimate action. But I needed to see it now. Need to prove she could be comfortable doing that, that this was more than just sex.

Rachel set the dress on the armchair in front of my desk and slipped off her shoes. Then she pulled at her skirt, shimming the fabric down till it pooled at her ankles. "Can we at least talk? It's kind of awkward with you just staring at me like that."

"Like what?"

"I dunno, you just …" Rachel turned around, as if the view of her ass was somehow less appealing than her front. "You have very intense eyes."

"I'm sorry?" I raised my eyebrow, not sure what she meant about my eyes.

"I mean, don't get me wrong, they're stunning. But I can't tell what you're thinking a lot of the time. So it'd be better for us to talk than for me to make assumptions about what you're thinking, right?"

I was thinking about how delicate her arms looked as her sleeves fell down.

"Do you like the dress?" I asked, clearing my throat as she began to put it on.

"Yes, it's the perfect color." Did that mean it was her favorite color? "It's almost the weekend, do you have plans?"

I didn't want to admit that my weekend plans, for every weekend, were boring. I worked far too late most days, which meant errands were only taken care of on the weekend. The most exciting thing I did was attend the occasional charity event. And she'd gone to those with me.

"I … don't have any plans. I typically … vacuum." Why was vacuuming the first thing that came to mind? I bet that other man had some interesting hobby, something he did on the weekend, something that would excite her.

"Vacuum?" Rachel repeated, a smile warming her voice. She pulled on the dress and turned back to me. She didn't look up as she tied the dress together, making a neat bow that I immediately wanted to undo. "I would've thought you used a maid service for that."

"Why would I pay someone to do something I'm perfectly capable of doing myself?" Her lips pulled into a big smile.

"I should've known you'd say that." Yes, that's right. Rachel did know me. Well. And sure, part of that was having worked together for so long and the fact that I was an open book. But part of it had to be the relationship I had been imagining, the relationship I was trying to solidify now. I just needed to remind myself of that every time I learn something new about Rachel and start freaking out.

"Ready?" I asked once she'd slipped her shoes back on. I tried to keep my voice confident, but something must have leaked through because she hesitated.

"Do you think we should go separately?"

"Separately?" I repeated.

"Yeah, well ... before, whenever we went somewhere, it could be excused as a work thing. But ..." She gestured at her clothes and mine. "This definitely doesn't look like a work thing."

"And?" I asked, uncertain of her point.

"And I'm pretty sure HR frowns on going out with employees."

"I don't care what they or anyone else thinks." I stepped closer, taking her hands in mine and resting my forehead against hers. Was this something I could push her on? Or would that make her rethink the possibility of us being in a serious relationship? Obviously, her concerns were valid but ... "If you're uncomfortable because people might see us, I can make sure no one says a thing. It's never been a problem before and I'll keep it that way. Or we can go separately like you said. But if you're uncomfortable because this is something we've not done before, something that puts us closer to the relationship I want, then ..." Then I want you to reconsider. I want you to test it out. I want ...

"I'll go first. You can meet me in the car when you're comfortable."

"No list of questions this time?" Rachel teased when we'd been seated and placed our drink orders with only casual conversation between us. And while she obviously didn't see the point of my questions, I wasn't about to abandon them. So I pulled my phone out and opened the notes app. But the file was much larger than last time and ...

"I know it's kind of an abuse of having access to your email, but it was driving me crazy not knowing what you were typing. So I kinda took a peek and ..."

"And filled in all your answers." She'd answered everything, even filled in some additional information like her family's names and the ages of her nieces. They'll turn one next month. And her favorite color was in fact plum. And having all that information at my fingertips felt ... warm, a soft warmth that relaxed my whole body.

"Thank you." It wasn't enough to express how grateful I was to have all this. But when I looked up at her, that smile, the light pink on her cheeks suggested she understood.

"You're welcome. I figured since I scheduled the vast majority of your life, it was only fair I give you at least that much information. Though I was surprised you knew my exact measurements."

"You shouldn't be surprised I've memorized your body. I'll memorize this just as well." I held up my phone to prove my point, then stored it away. I'd read through it before bed tonight, that way I'd have a little piece of her to fall asleep with.

"Well ... since all your questions are answered, it's time for mine."

"Of course." I shuffled in my seat, trying to run through the list of questions and figure out which she would ask first.

"So ..." She took a deep breath and my hands balled up into fists on my lap. "Who's your celebrity crush?"

What? That's what she asked?

"I ... Anne Hathaway, I suppose."

"A solid choice. But what's with the hesitation?"

"I don't go out to the movies often, so I wasn't sure that ..."

"That she still existed?" Rachel teased, laughing when I just shrugged in response. "She's still very popular, so she counts. Then next is pets. I mean, do you want them?"

I couldn't help but sigh. Why was she picking the questions I was least interested in? "No ferrets or birds or reptiles. Everything else depends."

"Depends on what?"

"Well, if we ..." I paused, catching the way she sucked on her lip, watching me intently. "If we want a dog, then we'd need a yard. If we want a cat, we'd need somewhere to put a litter box that couldn't be smelled from the main rooms. Rabbits ... I guess are fine either way."

"You've thought about that a lot, huh? Do you stay up all night scrolling through adoption sites?"

"No." She smirked and shrugged.

"I do. Especially corgis, they're just so cute, you know? But my apartment has a no pet rule."

"My place doesn't." It was just relevant information, but her eyes widened at the implication I hadn't meant. Living together was something I'd never considered. I had liked the way our relationship was before I knew it wasn't enough, I had no desire to change my life, my habits. But now ... I cleared my throat and asked about something tangentially related, "Do you have roommates?"

"No, thankfully my boss pays me well enough that I don't have to share." She winked and I unsuccessfully fought back a smile. "It's for the best, honestly. My last roommate *hated* me."

"Why?" For no good reason, I took offense at the possibility that some hated my Rachel. She was brightness, how could someone hate that?

"Oh, she just thought I was ..." Rachel trailed off, looking away as she sucked her lip. I couldn't tell how bad this hurt was. If it was me, with my regularly bland and stoic face, this sort of reaction would mean a lot. But Rachel was different. Her base reactions were so drastically different from mine, I didn't have a scale to go off of. So without any other idea, I took her hand in mine and gently squeezed.

"Tell me. Please."

She sighed and shook herself. "It's really not that big a deal. She just thought I was vain because I have lots of clothes and an obsessive skin care routine and I post on Instagram all the time. I mean, she's far from the first one to call me that, so it's whatever. Now I have a place of my own and can take up the whole bathroom counter, so it all worked out."

"Hmph, I like your clothes and your pictures," I murmured and Rachel tilted her head to the side, with a mischievous smile.

"Mr. Bleckard, have you been stalking my Instagram?"

I suddenly wanted, very much, for our waiter to come to take our order.

"Will you take one for me?"

"What?" I looked back when Rachel let go of my hand to dig into her purse. When she retrieved her phone, she stood and came over to me, putting my drink in my hand and moving my arm up.

"What?" I repeated as she shifted my other arm in front of me.

"Just humor me, okay?" Presumably satisfied with my position, she sat back down. I stayed still, uncertain of what she wanted from me. Obviously, she wanted a picture, but was this pose some kind of trend? Do I need to get an Instagram now to understand the things she wants?

"Hold your glass up just a little bit more." She leaned over as she spoke, holding up her phone to get another angle. I complied and her finger tapped the screen a few times. Then she sat back up and took a few more. She was smiling at her phone and, presumably, me. "Yeah, that's good. You really are quite — shit."

"Excuse me?" Was this just a different level of teasing? Or had my confusion over what she was doing translated into me looking unhappy?

"Morgan, my boy, what are you doing here?" My mother's voice cut through all the quiet chatter in the restaurant. And suddenly I understood Rachel's shift in attitude, her wide eyes and paling face. Crap.

"Mother," I muttered, trying to make it clear her presence was unwelcome without actually saying it. I stood and she immediately wrapped me into a suffocating hug. Not suffocating for any physical reason, but because she wore the most tear-inducing perfume and used it lavishly. I tried not to think about how that perfume was bought using the money I earned, but the irritation of being interrupted made me bitter. What the hell was she doing here?

"Oh, Rachel, hello." Mother's nose scrunched unpleasantly as she stepped away from me to see my dinner partner. Obviously Rachel wasn't who she expected. I could feel the words clawing at my throat, begging me to explain that Rachel was my date tonight and she should respect our peace.

"Good evening, Ms. Bleckard. How are you?" Rachel smiled politely, the smile she gave those irritating managers who tried to flirt their way out of trouble with her. They never managed the feat, but she always managed to keep that smile in place.

"I'm fine, but what are you two doing here?" Mother turned back to me, a deep-set frown already in place.

"Mr. Bleckard was kind enough to treat me to dinner to celebrate my work anniversary."

I hate that Rachel felt compelled to lie about what this was. Especially when this dinner meant so much to me. But I understood it. Mother was ... quick to look down on something and not exactly easy to sway over. She certainly wouldn't approve of me dating an employee, let alone my secretary. I didn't particularly care if she disapproved. I worked hard to please my mother, but I wouldn't budge on this. Rachel was the only woman I wanted and nothing could ever change that.

But if I said as much now, Mother would throw a fit, make Rachel uncomfortable, and ruin this chance I had to make her fall for me.

"This place is a little much for an employee, don't you think?" Mother half-whispered to me. Rachel tried to hide her snicker behind her drink.

"She deserves even more."

Rachel's snicker died immediately, red painting her cheeks as she looked away. Mother on the other hand stared at me, waiting for me to expand. She didn't wait long though. She at least knew me well enough to know there was no point in waiting for me to explain. She probably assumed something was going on, assumed I was using my secretary for sex, but she didn't ask. And for right now, that was good enough.

"Very well. Since it's not anything serious, I'll join you." Without another word, she sat to Rachel's right. I turned to Rachel, ice running through my veins, hoping she would have some magical words that would make my mother go away.

"That sounds lovely, ma'am."

Fuck.

Chapter Eleven

Morgan

After several excruciating hours, where Mother bombarded Rachel with questions about her schooling and background, Rachel and I were finally walking back to my car. Alone. We were finally alone and all of Rachel's body language was tense. Shit. Spending the evening with my mother was not what I had planned. It was too much too soon. I wouldn't be surprised if she quit as soon as we got in the car.

We were silent until the car doors shut us in and then Rachel burst out laughing. The kind of laugh where she doubled over and tears pooled at the corner of her eyes. And I didn't know how to interpret it.

"Oh my god, I'm sorry, Morgan. I know you love her, but your mom's just too much," Rachel managed to say through her laughter. "I really am sorry, I shouldn't laugh. But *god* she had *so* many questions. I guess that's where you get it from."

"No, I got my questions from counselors," I countered, a light chuckle escaping me now that I realized Rachel wasn't terrified and on the verge of running away from me. "But I should be the one to apologize. I have no idea how she knew I'd be there."

"She has access to your calendar, right? She probably saw you had reservations and couldn't help herself." Rachel was still giggling, but I groaned. She was right. Mother had probably looked at my calendar, assumed I was on a date, and felt the need to come to see who the lucky woman was. I guess I won't add things to my calendar from now on.

"I'm sorry," I muttered, not sure what else to say. I'd expected an evening of progress, of getting to know Rachel better and showing her that she could fall in love with me. All I had now was a train wreck of an evening.

"You looked ... a little put off when I said we were there for my work anniversary. Was that the wrong thing to say?" Her laughter was gone and I acutely missed the lightness of it. Especially given her question.

"Did I like it? No. But I understand. Mother means well, but given her expectations, that wouldn't have been the best time to tell her about our relationship." *If there will be a relationship.*

"Expectations?" Rachel repeated, shifting in her seat.

"No." I took her chin in my hand and forced her to look at me. "Don't do that."

"Don't do what?" She was trying to laugh, trying to play it off. She'd done that before, avoiding things when they got serious. That was something I'd need to address as a whole later. But for now, I'd start with just this one thing.

"Don't think that for a second that my mother's expectations change how I feel about you. Don't let them make you think less of yourself. Mother will get over whatever preconceived notions she has eventually, I'll make sure of it. But I didn't want her making a scene at the restaurant or making you uncomfortable. *That's* why I didn't say anything. Not because I was worried about what she'd thing."

"Oh." Rachel didn't say anything else, but she did stop shuffling and buckled up. With nothing else to add, I buckled myself and drove us out of the parking garage.

"Would you like me to come with you into the office?" I offered, making the proper turns to drive us back.

"Actually ..." Out of the corner of my eyes, I saw Rachel lick her lips. The action set a fire low in my gut. "We didn't get to talk much. And I hadn't gotten to the questions I was most curious about. So, if you — I mean, we could talk more at your place if you wanted. Or mine."

Everything inside me tensed. It felt like a test of my will.

"I'm not going back on my word."

"I know. I'm not asking you to." One corner of her lips tilted up. "I mean, I wouldn't complain if you did. But I really do wanna talk. There were a lot of questions on your list that were more discussions than something that I can answer on my own."

"All right, but I have conditions."

"Okay, hit me." Rachel turned in her seat to face me, smiling eagerly. God, this was going to get out of hand, wasn't it?

"You can't go into my bedroom." Beside me, she snickered, but I went on. "And you won't be taking a cab or anything back home. I'll drive you."

"Hmm, I guess I can agree to that." She rolled her eyes at me, but settled back in her seat, facing forward.

I spent the rest of the drive clutching the wheel, praying I had the capacity to have her in my home without wanting to devour her. I made a mental list of the pictures I would need to remove. One on the entryway table, two on the mantel. The more I thought of it, the more I realized how stupid it was. The pictures were all taken at company events, by the hired photographer. Technically, anyone in the office had access to them. They weren't for us, they just happened to be of us.

Thoughts still broiling, we reached my door. My keys shook as I unlocked the door and I cursed myself for my nerves. What was there to be nervous for? Besides those photos, there was nothing to be ashamed of. I just ... hoped she liked my place, hoped she could see herself there.

"Give me ... 20 seconds." Rachel's brow wrinkled, but I didn't dwell or wait for her to say anything. I ducked inside, closed the door, and got to work. The picture on the entryway table was from last year's Christmas party. She wore a full ball gown, green with gold stitching on the skirt. It was a candid photo of us in front of the Christmas tree, talking, her smiling up at me. I snatched the picture up, angry at myself for all the things I misconstrued, and made quick work of removing the other photos. They felt heavy in my hands. So I shoved that weight into my bedroom closet, unsure of what else to do with them. Then I covered them with a blanket for good measure.

I let out a shaky breath and strode back to the front door, opening it to Rachel, a small smirk pulling at her lips.

"Hide all your porn?" she teased.

"I don't have any porn, Rachel. You've more than satisfied those desires." It had been one of the questions on the list. One I hoped Rachel knew the answer to. One I thought was obvious, except ... earlier today, when she'd listed the different ... types of sex she wanted, I wanted it too. I'd never considered there to be other options, but as soon as she brought them up, I needed them.

"Really? You don't want more ..." she trailed off as she followed me inside. I couldn't tell if she stopped talking because of where the sentence would go or if it was a reaction to seeing my place. Instead of looking back to see, I focused on heading to the kitchen to pour us some wine.

"I ... I thought I was satisfied with the way things were before. But I won't know true satisfaction, till I know you're satisfied. Till we're both ..." In love. Those were the words that wanted to spill out of my mouth. I cleared my throat, and tried to start over. "Till we're both satisfied."

Wine poured, I joined Rachel back in the living room, where she'd made herself comfortable on the couch. Seeing her there, feet tucked under her, head resting on the back to watch me sit beside her, I was overwhelmed with comfort. Having her here, in my home, made it feel more like a home than it ever had before.

"Bathroom is that way, bedroom over there," I murmured, watching her look around the small condo.

"I kinda expected a penthouse, something that screamed excess wealth. But that really isn't your style, is it?"

"No. I live alone. There'd be no point."

"And you have better things to spend your money on, right?" I nodded. "Like your mom?" Another nod. "And me?"

Rachel shifted forward, the movement making her dress slide up, revealing enough skin to make my ears ring. Why did such a simple thing set me off?

"Am I wrong?" No, but bringing her here, so close to my bed, was.

"No, you're not wrong. I gave you my card, didn't I?"

"Yeah, I haven't had a chance to use it yet. Just wait until the weekend though, I'll do some real damage then." She poked at me with her glass and I couldn't help it, I smiled. And she returned it with a dazzling smile of her own. A smile that closed around my heart, tight but warm.

"So, what questions did you want to discuss?" I asked, trying to shake myself out of the moment, out of the overwhelming feelings that could drown me.

"Right, well ..." Rachel paused, taking long gulps from her glass before setting it aside. She looked me in the eyes, face a little flushed. "Since our whole issue was making shitty assumptions, I figured we should really talk about the whole 'what do you want out of our relationship' bit."

"I already told you what I wanted." Was it still unclear to her? How else could I say it without ripping open my chest and handing her my heart?

"Well, yeah, a little bit. But what does a serious relationship look like to you?"

"For one, it means I get to be the only one who fulfills your needs, physically and emotionally. I might need you to tell me exactly what you need sometimes, but that's what I want."

"So we'd go on dates?"

"Whenever you'd like."

"And we'd just … hang out at each other's place on lazy weekends? Binge-watch the Bachelor and snuggle?"

I bit back a groan. I don't know why the thought had never occurred to me, to have her in my space for no other reason than having her company, but I liked the sound of it. I liked it so much that I pulled her into me, settling her on my lap and kissing her forehead.

"Yes," I whispered and she nodded.

"Okay. And then, do you … are you expecting …" When she didn't continue, I squeezed her waist. "Right, so I'm almost 30, you know?"

"I'm aware." What did that have to do with anything?

"Yeah, so everybody, especially my mom, is expecting me to start settling down. So … yeah."

"Settling down as in marriage?" Rachel didn't look up at me, instead focusing on a button on my shirt. But she nodded, the motion small and a little uncertain. I let the idea sink in for a moment. Marrying Rachel. Promising to be with Rachel for the rest of my life. I didn't hate the idea. Though the thought of a wedding, with my mother insisting on things being her way, didn't sit well.

"Not right away. Just like … eventually. I'm not trying to settle down just because of the shit my mom and other people say. Though it'll definitely be nice to not have to hear that crap anymore. I just … I'm a little jealous, I guess, of the security that comes with that kind of relationship. And … yeah, being almost 30 does make me feel a little more … rushed to get it. Or at least be solidly working in that direction, you know?" Her words were quiet and sounded a little rehearsed, like she'd had this conversation in her head several times already. I pulled her in tighter, tucking her head under my chin.

"I admit, marriage isn't something I've given much thought to. Surprisingly, even my mother hasn't brought up the subject. But yes, that's something I'd like to work toward for you, with you." Holding her, I didn't feel the normal shame such emotional words would bring. They came out easy without hesitation. And it felt good. In my arms, Rachel nodded but didn't pull back to look at me, still fiddling with my shirt.

"Good, so we're on the same page there. Nice."

"Keep going," I said when she didn't continue, knowing there was more.

"Well, knowing we have the same end goal in mind, I — well, do you have any expectations for other milestones? Like moving in together? Would you think things weren't going well if we hadn't done that in X amount of time?"

I thought about it for a long moment and Rachel waited quietly for my answer. She didn't prod me after a few minutes of silence or give up on getting an answer altogether. She just waited, seemingly in her own world as she drew shapes along my chest.

"I think if it took longer than a year, I'd be worried something was ... going wrong. But that's more so for a check-in, not a sign of doom. You're always welcome here, as soon or as late as you want to come. Or we could find a new place together if you'd prefer." I pictured her clothes in the closet next to mine. Waking up to messy curls in my face. Sharing coffee over breakfast. Watching whatever show she put on even after she'd already fallen asleep just in case she asked me questions when she woke.

"Okay," Rachel murmured. Then, after a deep breath, she pulled out of my arms and sat up. "So, what would you bring with you on a desert island?"

Chapter Twelve

Rachel

"Look at this little guy!" I squealed, holding my phone out to Morgan. He took it and examined the little corgi pup. He didn't outright smile at me like he'd done earlier, but his features softened. Which was enough for me to assume that he liked the dog.

It might be the wine talking or our earlier conversation, but I think I'm getting better at reading Morgan's reactions. He was a stoic man, so small things, like a tense jaw or a tilted lip, meant more. I'd just not been looking close enough. And now I was because ... well I spent the whole work day thinking about Morgan and what he wanted and what I wanted and why warning bells went off. And while I didn't get any work done today, I did realize that as appealing as a serious, fully committed relationship was, it scared me too. It was new, I didn't really know what I was doing, and I could get hurt so easily. I mean, that's what happened with my last boyfriend. Even if that was in high school.

But that fear started to ease when I saw Morgan's closet. I mean, are the clothes he bought me beautiful and overly expensive? Yes. But they were also exactly my taste and size. And the list he made, which I know I shouldn't have peeked at but my curiosity was killing me, was from a counselor site to build a good foundation with your partner. It was all so ... damn cute. I never thought I'd say it, but Morgan Bleckard was cute. He did all this cute shit for me and I'd never noticed just because he hadn't said anything. I wonder if that was some sort of toxic masculinity thing, like the only emotion he could express was sexual desire and everything else was repressed.

So, yeah, I'm definitely breaking up with Greg. Even if Morgan hadn't been in the picture, that baby comment was a sure sign we wouldn't work long term anyways. And then after that was taken care of, Morgan and I would …

"You really want a dog that badly?" Morgan asked.

"I do. … But don't buy one for me." I tried to give him a stern look, but a smile broke through anyways. Morgan turned his head away and I translated it as a blush. How could I not? In any other situation, Morgan wouldn't back down or look away. But he looked away from me, like he was trying to regain control of himself.

"Give me some credit. I wouldn't just get you a dog without making a plan." He was quiet for a long moment, before leaning back into me and asking, "Did you post that picture you took?"

"Oh, no, I wouldn't post it without showing you first." I pulled up the photo of Morgan and I had to say, it really was a good picture. I'd angled it so his whisky glass blocked most of his face, giving it a vague, cool aesthetic. It would be a very nice "soft launch" photo. Not that I planned my Instagram *that* much, but it would still make a good post.

"You can't see my face," Morgan pointed out.

"Yeah, but like, that's kind of a thing. It makes you look suave, don't you think?"

Morgan huffed, but didn't further elaborate on his feelings, which I took to mean he didn't mind if I posted it.

"How should I caption it, hmm? Maybe 'benefits of dating a rich man'?" Morgan huffed and squeezed the arm around my waist. "Fine, fine. I'll just do some drink emojis."

"What about 'mine'?" Morgan's voice was so soft and gruff, I almost thought I imagined that he said that. But when I looked up at him, he was sucking on his lip, like he could take back the words he just said. Then he grumbled, "It's late, let's get you home."

I pressed the little check mark to post, then stared at the time. He was right, it was late. Too late in the night to push him about that comment and what he meant by it.

"Okay. But since it is so late, I think I should call a cab." Behind me, Morgan tensed. I could just picture his face, lips tilting down, brow furrowed, looking generally displeased. When I turned to look at him, I couldn't help but laugh, which only deepened his frown.

"We already agreed that I would take you home."

"Yeah, but that was hours ago. You normally get in earlier than me, so I'm sure it's already past your bedtime."

"I don't mind losing sleep over you. It wouldn't be the first time." Morgan's grip around me tightened again and I couldn't help but wonder what kind of loss of sleep he was thinking of. When we'd gone back to hotel rooms late at night or when he was simply thinking of me?

"Then what if ..." I trailed off, not sure of what I was about to suggest. We'd never slept together. I mean, innocently slept together. Morgan had always seemed like the kind of man who valued his personal space first and foremost. So with that assumption in mind, even when we were out of town for conferences, I always made sure I had a room to go back to.

"I'll take the couch. Give me a second and I'll get the bedroom ready for you and ... something comfortable to sleep in." Morgan shifted me off him and strode to the bedroom. It didn't sound like an invitation to follow, but I did anyways.

Morgan's room was modern, simple, but without many personal touches or color. The only picture he had was one of him and his mother on the dresser. His college graduation, probably. He looked a little miserable and hot, but his mom looked proud.

I sat on the edge of the bed, watching as Morgan pulled out a white under shirt and a pair of boxer briefs and set them on my lap. He looked me up and down, jaw tight, then turned to leave. But I caught his wrist.

"Morgan, get in bed with me."

"No, thank you."

"Oh come on, I'm not going to jump you while you're asleep or any-thing. I'll keep my hands to myself, promise." I set the clothes aside and stood.

"Are you trying to torture me, Rachel?"

"No." I pulled at the string tying my dress together and let it fall open. Then shifted my shoulders to shimmy it down my arms. It didn't fall smoothly, of course, but Morgan's eyes were glued to me. They bounced around my body like he wasn't sure what he should look at first. "Do you want me to keep going?"

"Yes," he said, the sound part growl, part whimper.

I reached behind me and unhooked my bra. It fell to the floor, shortly followed by my underwear. I didn't really do anything, I honestly wouldn't have the first clue on how to put on a show. I just watched Morgan's eyes turn dark and hungry. Watched his Adam's apple bob when I stood. Watched his dick stiffen.

And then I turned around and slid the clothes he'd given me on. *His* clothes. They smelled a bit like him, and not just his soap but something that was innately him. I couldn't help but pull the shirt up and take a deep breath. When I looked over my shoulder, Morgan was frozen in place, just one, slightly miserable moan escaping his lips.

"I'd offer to help, but I assume you'd refuse me." I tossed down the sheets and climbed into bed. Once I was settled, I looked back to Morgan, who hadn't moved, hands clenched at his side.

"You're correct."

"If I wasn't here, would you take care of yourself?"

"No."

"Why not?" We hadn't had sex since … Thursday, maybe. Which admittedly wasn't that long ago, but it was long past our average. Had he really not at least jerked off since then?

"I'd rather the next time I came be inside you. Preferably like you are now, in my bed."

Fuck yes, that sounded good. I missed Morgan's dick, specifically having it in me.

I shifted again so that I was propped up against his headboard and slid the sheets down past my knees. And, keeping eye contact with Morgan, I grazed my fingers down from my collarbone. His breath hitched when I reached the swell of my breast, so I stayed there, tracing light circles over my nipples.

"Do you want a preview? Of me coming in your bed? Maybe while you tell me what you normally think about when you jack off?"

Something inside Morgan must've snapped because within seconds his clothes were ripped off. I quite literally heard a seam tear. And then he was climbing on top of me. He yanked me down so I was lying beneath him, his thighs on either side of my hips. He leaned forward, gripping the headboard with one hand and his cock with the other. His cock. Fuck, he was so hard and ready for me. Just the sight of it had me licking my lips. I missed his taste.

"Behave, dear. We're not touching each other. This is as close as you're getting to my cock. I can't touch you in this bed without wanting all of you, understand?"

"Yes," I breathed, my nipples hardening further. "But isn't that all the more reason why you should come all over me now? Release some of that tension?"

Morgan cursed, letting go of his dick to jerk my shirt over my breasts. His hand stilled in the wrinkled fabric, watching as I started pinching my nipples.

"Get a hand down there, play with that needy little clit." I complied and the sound Morgan made was sweet fucking music to my ears. "The first thing I think about is eating that sweet cunt like I did this morning. It always starts with wanting your taste. You taste so fucking perfect, it's never enough."

I teased my clit with slow circles, hypnotized by the frantic way Morgan was stroking himself. My words came out breathy as I told him what I thought about. "I like a little more build-up to my fantasies. Heavy stares between long meetings, being surrounded by people and you finding a way to touch me in a way that sets me on fire. And when you can't take it anymore, you whisk me into your office, whisper that you need me."

"I do."

"And that little neck thing you do, where you lick and suck. Like you're just barely holding back from giving me a hickey, marking me as yours." He grunted in reply, his breath coming in uneven and heavy waves already. "But yeah, once you have me all worked up and dripping, I think of you cleaning me up."

"Christ, Rachel. Put a finger in that pussy. Stretch it out for me, stroke that spot that makes your eyes roll back."

"Morgan," I whimpered, following his command and crooking my finger to stroke my G-spot.

"And then after I've had my fill of you, after you've made a mess all over my face, I'll pull you onto my lap, have you ride me. I barely stopped myself from doing that today. You really wanted me to break, huh?"

"Yes. But can you blame me? You make me feel so goddamn good."

"That's right, dear. And I'll make you feel good every damn time once you're mine. Let you ride my cock whenever you want. Nice and slow to get that build-up you like so much. Put another finger in, dear, I know you need it."

I added a second finger, pressing my palm down, trying to add friction against my clit. I closed my eyes, tight, trying to remember what it felt like when he filled me. How it felt to stretch for him.

"But as much as you like that slow build, you love when I lose it, don't you? When I'm so out of my mind with want, I just take you over my desk and ram into you, hard and fast."

and fast." "Please," I whined. I quickened the pace of my fingers inside me and tugged at my nipple with my other hand. Above me, Morgan stroked himself harder, a bead of pre-come shining on his head. I wanted to clean it off.

"Morgan." Heat twisted inside me deliciously, tangling tight but not tight enough.

"Rachel, please."

Shit. Warmth flooded my hand at the same moment Morgan leaned over me, spreading his own warmth across my breast. We both stayed there for a moment as our breaths slowed back to normal. It was far from the most intense orgasm I've had with Morgan, but ... it was so different from what we normally did. It filled a different spot, a different need.

With my clean hand, I reached up and cupped Morgan's cheek. He inhaled sharply, those bright eyes refocusing on me. The look was soft, almost loving. And then Morgan shook his head and the moment was gone.

"I'll get a washcloth, wait here," he murmured, climbing off of me and to the en suite. Carefully cupping my hands around Morgan's come, I got up and joined him. He was standing at the sink, the water on, towel in hand, but hadn't moved to get the cloth wet. Instead, he was staring at the water, eyes lost.

"I know you told me to wait, but I need to wash my hands anyways. And pee," I said, after clearing my throat. Morgan's eyes met mine, slowly regaining focus. He nodded, wetting the cloth before handing it to me and walking out. I watched for a second as he busied himself with getting dressed before turning off the lights and climbing into bed.

Huh.

I quickly washed myself up, peed, and snuggled up behind Morgan. I wrapped one hand around his stomach and pulled close. Then I kissed his back.

"How come you only call me dear when we're … in the moment?" I'd spoken so quietly, I almost thought he didn't hear me. But when he stiffened, pulling away from me, I knew he had.

"I'm sorry, it won't happen again."

"What?" He'd pulled away so there were a few inches of space between us, but I could still tangle my fingers in his shirt.

"I'm sorry," he mumbled again.

"Morgan, no. I like it. Why would you think I wouldn't?" Morgan just shrugged. "Well … I do. Like it, I mean. And I'd like you to use it outside of sex, I mean if you'd like."

Morgan's shoulders relaxed. "All right, dear."

"There are a lot of things you hold back on, aren't there?" He shrugged again but remained silent. So I tugged on his shirt and asked, "Why did you never tell me about the clothes?"

"There was no reason to, you never needed them."

"I would've liked them, even if I didn't need them. You picked them out, that's enough for them to mean something." I couldn't really say how I knew Morgan's silence wasn't his usual, quiet thinking, but I knew. "I find it easier to talk like this. When it's dark and we're holding on to each other. I don't want you to hold back any of your feelings. I wanna know about everything I didn't see before, everything I missed. And maybe talking about it like this will be easier."

Without turning, Morgan reached for my hand on his back and pulled until I was up against him. He held my hand, fingers entwined, pressed to his chest.

"I bought them because I thought you would like them. Then I had no reason to give them to you, then I considered they might be a burden, then I started to think that maybe I was wrong and you wouldn't even like them."

I nuzzled my face into his back. "I do like them. Thank you for getting them, thank you for thinking of me, for caring for me. Tell me more."

"When you were gone in the fall, for that wedding, I missed you. You'd left a sweater in the office, so I … took it home. Just to have something of yours. It … it smelt like you, for the first few days."

"I'm sorry. I missed you too. Would you have gone with me, for a week of wedding activities, if I asked?"

"Of course."

"That would've been nice. It kinda sucked watching all my friends get picked up by their guys after the bachelorette party. And babysitting my drunk friend after a fight with her boyfriend wasn't that fun either. It would've been nice to have you there for all that."

Morgan squeezed my hand, pulling it up to kiss before resting it back on his chest. We were quiet again for a moment. And I thought that was as far as we'd get tonight. It was enough, it was so much, more than he'd ever opened up about before. But when he pulled me closer, shaking, I knew there was more.

"I want you to pick me. To be mine. I want it so fucking badly. I'm scared of losing you." He was holding me so tightly, like saying the words physically hurt him.

"Morgan, turn around." I tugged the hand he was holding, not expecting him to do as I asked. But then he did and my heart … squeezed. There were tears in his eyes. And while he let me wipe them away, he didn't look at me. Instead, he kept his eyes downcast. That was until I started speaking.

"Even if I gave you the answer you wanted right now, you'd doubt it in the morning. You'd think I was saying it in the heat of the moment or that you made me feel pressured. When I give you my decision, there won't be a single doubt in my mind or yours. But thank you for telling me how you feel. Thank you for caring about me so much." I stroked his cheek until his tension eased, then kissed his forehead. When I looked back at him, a soft smile pulled at his lips. "Feel better?"

"Yes, dear." Morgan leaned over to kiss my forehead before gripping my waist and flipping me over. He then pulled me into him, nuzzling his face into my neck. "Now go to sleep. Or we'll be late for work. And your boss hates tardiness."

"Yes, sir."

Chapter Thirteen

Morgan

I woke up with Rachel's arm around me, her soft warmth pressed against my back, and felt … settled. Last night, after watching her orgasm in my bed and calling out my name, something inside me broke.

No, broke wasn't the right word. Scattered. I'd become scattered, all my emotions all over the place and I had no clue how to start picking them up. But Rachel did. She spoke softly, held me, and didn't look away from my tears. It was the first time I didn't feel ashamed to have cried. And that alone was enough to confirm I loved her.

I took the arm that was wrapped around me and held her tightly.

I loved Rachel Conrad. She was the first and only woman I have ever or will ever love.

And I couldn't tell her. Not now, not when it could be interpreted as too much too soon. She'd specifically said she didn't want to rush things, she just wanted to be on the right path. Telling her might send her into the arms of another man. Like hell was I taking that chance.

But not telling her … The whole issue between us was because she thought I didn't care in the first place. So I needed to strike some kind of balance.

The clothes. She liked those, and didn't seem to think they were too much. What else could I buy for her, what else could I do for her that would be on the same level?

"Morgan," Rachel murmured behind me, hand tightening in my shirt as she pulled herself even closer.

"Yes, dear?" It was liberating knowing I could call her that, knowing she didn't find it weird or clingy.

"Do we have time to stop by my place before work?" Her voice had a gravelly aspect to it, something I'd never heard before. That combined with the way her breath tickled my neck, I was one temptation away from fucking her into the bed.

"If we go now, yes. Just give me a few minutes to get ready." I quickly pulled away from Rachel and the temptation of her. When I stood, Rachel grumbled and it became physically impossible not to turn back and kiss her head. Her hair was a mess of flattened curls and static. It was cute.

Rachel hummed and, with her eyes still closed, reached up to kiss my cheek. Then she crashed down and curled up again. I went about my regular morning routine, finding myself smiling for no reason other than knowing Rachel was there. And I didn't even feel silly about it.

Then, as I was brushing my teeth, Rachel came in and peed. This woman, who had said changing in the same room as me would be too intimate, was peeing right next to me. Rachel seemed to notice this too, because after she'd finished her business, she sat up straight, eyes wide.

"Oh my god, I'm so sorry. I just — I guess I was half asleep. I'll give you your space back. Sorry," she murmured, quickly wiping up and moving to leave. I put my arm out to stop her.

"You don't have to be sorry. I'm happy to share my space with you."

Rachel licked her lips, nodding before looking up at me. "You were kinda giving me this weird look."

"I was surprised. You didn't want to change in front of me yesterday."

"Yeah, but that was before ..." Before I cried in front of her. Apparently, that intimate act meant she was comfortable peeing in front of me. And oddly enough, it was worth it.

I let her go and dug through the drawers to pull out an extra toothbrush. I set it on the counter for her and we started a slow rhythm of washing up and getting ready for the morning. Rachel borrowed a pair of sweats to wear along with my other clothes she slept in and then we were out the door.

It wasn't exactly a quiet ride on the way to Rachel's. She'd plugged in her phone with directions and took control of the music, playing some pop music I wasn't familiar with. She sang along, voice still gravely from sleep, and occasionally would stop to tell me about something she saw on her phone or give different directions than the app, because supposedly it was taking me the long way around.

This. This was how it would be in the morning. Songs that would likely be stuck in my head all day. Her telling me about things I didn't particularly care about or could even follow. And leaning over during stop lights to kiss her forehead.

If things worked out, I could have mornings like this for the rest of my life.

No, that was thinking too far ahead. I needed to concentrate on the here and now. Come up with my next steps.

"You can park right there." Rachel pointed out a spot in the garage and I dutifully followed her instruction. She quickly got out of the car and I … just sat there. Was I supposed to wait here or follow? Did she have things in her home she wanted to clear before having me over? Did she even want me to see her place at all? Was that something normally done after more time dating?

A knock on my window made me jump and I turned to see Rachel, a teasing smile lighting her face as I rolled down the window.

"Are you coming? Or is sitting in the car your way of telling me to be quick?"

I grumbled in reply and Rachel laughed, stepping out of the way so I could join her.

"Your picture did very well on the Gram, Mr. Bleckard." Rachel held out her phone for me to see. The photo had several hundred likes, though I had no clue how that compared to her average photos, and about a dozen comments, only two of which were displayed. The first was something about sharing the "deets" and the other from a Gracie, whom I'm pretty sure was Rachel's sister-in-law, saying, "This is him" with several question and exclamation marks.

Before I could ask what the comment meant, Rachel slid her phone into her bag and traded it for a set of keys. We stopped in front of a door with a welcome mat where the O in welcome was a four-leaf clover. Did she have a mat for every holiday? If we had a home together, would it be decorated for every holiday? Lights and decoration everywhere?

"So you can't judge me for my clutter, okay? I have a lot of stuff and it kinda just ends up everywhere," Rachel said as she unlocked the door. And before I had a chance to assure her I would do no such thing, the door was open.

Clutter wasn't the word I would use to describe Rachel's apartment. It was full and bright. Tapestries and some sort of yarn work covered the walls, fairy lights balled into glass jars sat on bookshelves, and throw blankets were strewn across the back of the couch. It was a home that was lived in, cared for in a way a home was meant to be. In comparison, my place was just where I slept, nothing close to a home. I hadn't decorated or put any thought into the furniture I bought. I'd thoroughly underestimated the effect such consideration could have.

"Okay, so I'm gonna need like … 20 — 30 minutes tops. Is that all right?" Rachel set her keys in a bowl on the entryway counter and started toward her open bedroom.

"Take your time, Rachel. We don't have any meetings this morning, so I'm sure your boss won't mind if you're a little late." Unsure of what else to do, I sat on the couch, sinking into the deep cushions. From her room, Rachel poked her head out, already undressed.

"Mr. Bleckard, are you teasing me?" she giggled.

"Get dressed, Rachel." There was more warning in my voice than I intended. But her naked collar bone, arm partly covering her breast, it was too early in the morning for me to be this close to breaking.

"Oh, all right. Bathrooms on the right and help yourself to whatever's in the kitchen. I hope you're not expecting me to be the cook in this relationship. I'm very rarely in the mood to cook or bake unless it's a holiday thing." Rachel went back into her room, music playing as soon as she was out of sight.

The way she talked about our relationship, like it had officially started, spurred me to do something moderately presumptuous. I went to her bathroom and took a picture of every product she had so I could order her a set to keep at my place. I even took pictures of the things that were barely touched, either because they weren't used often or because she didn't end up liking them. If I got the chance to have her at my palace again, I wanted her to have everything she needed to stay there.

And when that was done, I opened the search bar for doctors able to perform a vasectomy with short notice. Because it was something I could do for her on my own, because it would keep her safe. And because I was grasping at straws and maybe a little surgery would do me good. Plus I'd already taken sex off the table for the next week, so what did it matter?

Chapter Fourteen

Rachel

We ended up being exactly 32 minutes late to work. Which ordinarily wouldn't have been a big deal, but today some asshole who was a face for the company decided to show his face on Twitter. So Morgan's been busy with the firing and subsequent PR announcements, while I've already gone through 100 resumes HR passed along.

So, you know, a super fun morning. Only to be made more fun by Ms. Bleckard's sudden appearance. *Second* sudden appearance.

"Hello, Ms. Bleckard, lovely seeing you again. Mr. Bleckard's in the middle of an important phone call, but I'll send him a message to let him know you're here. Can I get you something to drink in the meantime?" I got up and turned to the drink station behind my desk, ignoring Ms. Bleckard's huff. She reminded me a lot of Emily Gilmore, with the same scratchy-looking skirt suits, the same air of importance, the same poor treatment of employees. Any second now she was going to go on a tirade about —

"I'm sure whatever he's doing isn't as important as talking to his mother," she grumbled, moving towards the door. I quickly stepped in front of her, blocking the door and holding out the first drink I could grab, which happened to be a Diet Coke. Pretty sure that wouldn't be within her refined palate.

"It really is an important call, ma'am. He had to let go of one of the VPs due to inappropriate behavior and is handling some PR calls now. I'm sure that he'll wrap the call up as soon as he can, but an unexpected interruption might ... make things worse."

Morgan took after his mother in regard to facial reactions. There wasn't even a twitch as she looked down at the soda in my hand and turned for the couch a few feet from my desk. "I'll take a water."

ed her water and returned to my desk. I sent Morgan a message about his mom and was quickly given a one-word reply. "Understood." Hm, knowing what I know about him now, Morgan probably expected his mother to come by but wasn't happy about it. I wonder if he was hoping we could do lunch again. Probably not given how busy he was, but ... maybe. I'd like to.

"Morg— Mr. Bleckard will be with you as soon as possible, ma'am." Shit, that got an eyebrow raise. Just a few days of calling him Morgan and I was already defaulting to it. God, I hope he doesn't come out and accidentally call me dear. Though I bet the look on his mother's face would be hysterical.

"Rachel, what is your relationship with my son?"

"He's my employer, ma'am." Not technically a lie. It'd probably upset him if I outright lied about our relationship. But he understood why I'd lied about yesterday's dinner, so this should be fine.

Surprisingly, Ms. Bleckard huffed and rolled her eyes at my response. "Fine, I'll ask it plainly then. Are you fucking my son?"

Had I been drinking something, it would've gotten all over my computer. Hell, even without something to drink, it felt like I was choking on the air. I expected her to press the issue, but not like that.

"I'm sorry, what?" Maybe if I feigned innocence, she'd back down.

"You heard me. Are you fucking my son or not? He certainly wouldn't take just any employee out to that sort of place for dinner. You're pretty enough for *that* sort of relationship, I suppose."

We weren't even technically together yet and already his mother was giving me a headache. Great.

"Well, ma'am, no. I'm not sleeping with your son. I'm not particularly interested in *that* kind of relationship at my age." There. That wasn't a lie *and* I was keeping my cool. I was so cool about the situation, I wasn't praying for Morgan to step out or for the phone to ring. Actually, I was begging.

"What? You think you're too good for that? My son is handsome, a billionaire even, what else could you possibly want?"

What the hell was this woman? First, she was disgusted by the possibility that I was sleeping with Morgan, now she was insulted that I wasn't.

"Well, for one thing, love. I'm not looking to hookup with anyone anymore, I'm looking for ... someone to marry, someone I can trust to be in my future. Surely you want something like that for your son, something more than just fucking his secretary."

"Are you implying that my Morgan isn't marriage material?" These wild jumps had to be a Bleckard family thing. It was giving me déjà vu to when I told Morgan I was quitting. Just one surprising jump to another. None of which I could see coming.

"Ma'am, you seemed ... put off by the idea that I was sleeping with him. So why would it matter if I wanted to marry him or not?"

Ms. Bleckard opened her mouth to reply but promptly shut it when the door behind me opened. Morgan frowned at his mother and she had the decency to look away, ashamed.

"Mother, what are you doing here?" Morgan's tone was short, probably irritated to be interrupted like this, with me almost yelling at his mother.

"Well after our call this morning, I was worried. Is she the reason? She claimed you're not together. Did she reject you?" His mother stood, arms crossed, eyes narrowed at me.

"Mother, whether Rachel wants a relationship with me or not is between her and me. I expect you to respect that. And your certainly not helping my case by bombarding her with questions at work." Morgan stared down at his mother the way he stared down at people who tried to go back on a deal. It was intimidating, but also kinda ... hot. He respected the hell out of this woman, but he wouldn't let her disrespect me. Which like, duh, that should be expected in a good relationship, but seeing it in action made a real impact. I'd reward him with a nice blow job if he'd let me.

But unfortunately, his mother had an equally strong, no backdown attitude.

"I just don't see why she would reject a man of your caliber. She certainly can't do better," Ms. Bleckard said, crossing her arms. I mean ... she was right. If you were breaking things down in a pro-con list, Morgan for sure won out.

"I'm doing my best to convince her of that, but you will have no involvement in her decision, Now, I have an appointment to get to, so if you'd like to talk some more, do it on the way to the car."

"Appointment?" Ms. Bleckard and I said at the same time. I cleared his schedule earlier today of any regular meetings to give him breathing room to deal with this morning's fiasco. And I definitely haven't added anything since.

"There's nothing on your calendar today. That's why I came over," Morgan's mom echoed my thoughts and I found myself nodding along. Maybe we could get along some times.

"I didn't put it on the calendar, because of your tendency to snoop," Morgan grumbled. With a gentle hand on her back, he pushed his shocked mother forward and toward the elevators. Then, before he was out of earshot, he turned to me and said, "I've already set up my out-of-office email, but if anyone calls, you can let them know I'll be back early tomor-row."

"Oh, okay." And then he was gone. And I was a little disappointed I didn't get a kiss goodbye.

Well, at least now I was free for the evening to talk to Greg.

Schools were gross. The air was stale and even the office, which didn't seem to have any children present, was sticky. Thankfully I didn't have to wait long for Greg to show up.

I was hoping he'd be done for the day since school had already let out, but apparently, he had more work to get done and insisted we talk in his classroom, which was, of course, just as sticky and stale as the office. And he didn't have any other adult chairs, so I was stuck on a plastic chair that practically cried under my weight.

Well, maybe me breaking this seat will make this break up easier. Greg might be so busy laughing at me, he wouldn't feel hurt.

"So Greg ..."

Ugh, I'd practiced this speech since Morgan left work and again on the car ride here. How did I still not have the right words for this?

"Yes, Rachel?" He barely looked up from the paper he was working on, which did make me feel a tad justified for this impromptu break-up.

"Right. So we talked about working towards exclusivity the other day and I know that's not going to work between the two of us. So, you know, no point in the two of us going out again."

"What?" Greg asked, finally looking up at me, shock paling his face.

"Well, it's just —"

"Was the sex that bad?" he interrupted. And well ... it wasn't that great, but that was more because I was comparing him to Morgan than a reflection on his skills. Or maybe it was. Maybe I was giving him too much of the benefit of the doubt.

"No, I just don't think —"

"It's that other guy, isn't it?" He was raising his voice now. And not letting me speak. Great. But also, point proven, no need to feel bad about this.

"Well, our values align more, so it —"

"Values?" he huffed, crossing his arms and leaning back in his properly sized chair. "It's your boss, isn't it? Sounds like your value is attached to his bank account."

"Excuse me? Did you just call me a gold digger?" I laughed. This week was just chock-full of ridiculous arguments. Why not add dumb accusations on top of it?

"Well, if the shoe fits. You're already vain as hell, might as well go after money too. I guess a teacher wouldn't make enough to keep you looking the way you do."

"Oh my god. You know what, fuck you. And fuck your stupid assumptions and judgements." Half laughing, half burning with anger, I stood, grabbing my bag and knocking the tiny chair back in the process.

"You know, I actually tried to break up with him because I thought you'd be a better fit. Crazy, right? I was thinking about quitting my job, leaving him, and all his riches, so I could get with someone serious. Someone like you. And then he practically begged me not to. And that wasn't even what really convinced my dumbass that he was the one. It was you saying I would change my mind about kids. Seriously, what the fuck? As a teacher, surely you know the effect of what being an unwanted kid has. So, you know, good bye, don't call. Best of luck finding someone who isn't vain and wants kids. Just a hint, next time a girl wants to walk away, maybe don't imply she's a gold digger and talk to her if you really want her to say."

I left Greg stunned, mouth wide open. Good. Gold digger my ass.

Chapter Fifteen

Rachel

It was three o'clock on Friday and I still hadn't told Morgan I was ready to take our relationship to the next level or become steady or whatever the fuck we were gonna call it. But every time I'd gone into his office, which had been five times now, I chickened out. I knew this was going to be a good thing, I knew that I would fall in love with him, I knew he wouldn't hurt me. So why the fuck was it so hard to get the words out?

All right. One more time, I'll get it out this time for sure.

I knocked on Morgan's door and he immediately called for me to come. Once in, he eyed me carefully. Probably wondering if I was gonna beg him to fuck me again. Which didn't sound like a bad alternative. Sex or talking about my feelings? Such a hard choice.

"I just wanted to let you know that ..." *I broke up with Greg and I'm ready to be with you.* This was getting stupid. Was I really that scared of getting hurt? Or was there something else bugging my self-consciousness? Shit, should I go to therapy?

"Yes, dear?"

"I was wondering if you wanted to come with me to visit my brother and his family this weekend?" The words were out of my mouth quicker than I could think better of them. And by the look on Morgan's face, he was confused by the invitation too.

"Go with you to visit your brother?" Morgan repeated.

"Yes. The twins' birthday is next month, so I was gonna go over and help Gracie mail out the invitations. She's doing this weird DIY glitter thing and I just thought …" This was stupid? What would he do while I was helping Gracie? Talk to my brother? And how was I going to introduce him? As my boyfriend? I was having enough trouble telling *him* that, how would I say it to my family?

"Yes. I'd love to. Should I meet you at your place beforehand?" Morgan pulled out his phone, already marking the event in his calendar.

"Oh yeah, that'd be good."

"Time?"

"Umm … noon, I guess."

"And you said you typically bring a change of clothes, should I do that too? Or will wearing something I don't mind staining be fine?"

Oh god, so many questions. I'd almost forgotten how thorough Morgan was when it came to planning shit.

"Probably both. The stains are normally throw up, so not exactly something you wanna sit around in for hours on end."

"Understood." Morgan nodded, continuing to type notes into his phone. "And will we be eating lunch or dinner there?"

"Um … maybe? This isn't like a formal thing, we'd mostly just be hanging out with them. Normally if I end up staying late, we just get delivery or something."

"And should I bring something?" Oh. Something about this question made it click that taking him to see my family, even if it was just my brother, was a very big deal. Especially since we hadn't technically started this relationship. No wonder he was taking this so seriously, to him this was a chance to solidify the fact that he should be my partner. Even though he sorta already won that role.

I could just say it now, clear up the confusion. And then there'd be less pressure on both of us. But did I get those words out? Nope.

"No, you don't have to bring anything, really. It's not that big of a deal, it'll be just the four of us … well six with the kids. And honestly, Chase will probably just be relieved to have a grown adult to talk to that he's not related or married to."

"All right. I look forward to it." Morgan looked back down at his phone, inputting the last of the information, then turning back to the computer. When I didn't move to leave though, he raised a brow. "Is there anything else?"

"No, sorry. I'll go back to work." This would be fine. He'd get to know the best part of my family and then I can tell him when we get back. Perfect plan.

Chapter Sixteen

Morgan

Rachel's been acting strange. Not strange enough that I think she found out about the vasectomy, but still … odd. She was jittery, either talking a mile a minute or saying nothing. It made for a confusing drive out to her brother's place.

The quiet was fine by me, at least for now. I'd spent all yesterday hiding an ice pack under my desk, but thankfully today was mostly pain free. So long as no one kicked my dick, my secret was safe. Not that it was a secret, but I couldn't find the words or the moment to tell Rachel. A week ago, I wouldn't have thought much about telling her. If it came up, I'd mention it, if not, then it didn't matter. But now … now I realized what it really meant to her. Which, of course, had the effect of making all my words stick in my throat.

"You can just park in the driveway," Rachel instructed, a knee bouncing. It made me wonder why she was so nervous. Surely I wasn't the first man she introduced her brother to. And she'd repeated, several times now, that this was just a casual get together. So why couldn't she stay still?

Parked, Rachel immediately hopped out of the car and made her way into the home. I took my time grabbing our bags before following Rachel inside. Inside the door, three people stared at me with wide and possibly eager eyes. Except Rachel, she still looked rather nervous.

"What're those?" she murmured, nodding to the gifts in one bag instead of introducing me.

"Blocks for your nieces and wine and dessert for the adults." For the first time since I picked her up, she smiled. A soft, sweet smile. Beside her, Chase rolled his eyes, then held out a hand to take the bag.

"Nice to meet you, man. Chase. Rachel said, and I quote, 'to act cool'. But seeing as she isn't even able to make proper introductions, that's already out of the question." Switching the gifts to his other hand, Chase shook my hand. Then Rachel promptly elbowed his side.

"What the fuck, Chase?" Rachel half yelled, half whispered.

"What? It's, like, my prerogative to embarrass you when you bring a guy over. And you haven't brought anybody over since, like, high school. So I've got a lot of time to make up for," Chase teased before walking towards what appeared to be the kitchen. Rachel followed right on his heels, arguing with him.

"Don't mind them, they're always like that. I'm Gracie by the way. Nice to meet you, Morgan. Rachel's told me a lot about you." Gracie shook my hand and, when the look on my face probably read as sheer panic, added with a giggle, "Good things, of course."

Right. A week ago, Rachel thought our relationship was exclusively about sex. Which meant the things Rachel told her sister-in-law were ...

I tried to clear my throat, but still barely managed to get words out. "Thank you for having me on such short notice."

Gracie smiled and quiet set in. The kind of quiet that I knew would get uncomfortable quickly if I didn't offer up any small talk. And while normally, I wouldn't bother at all, this was Rachel's family and coming off as a dick wasn't an option.

"I wasn't —"

"Morgan, I told you you didn't have to bring anything," Rachel said, joining us back in the entryway for just long enough to grab my arm and drag me into the kitchen. There, Chase was pouring us each a glass of the wine and the cheesecake I'd brought was already open with a large bite missing.

"It'd be rude not to bring something," I murmured, accepting the glass Chase offered.

"Okay, fine. But you got the girls 150 blocks. Each."

"I figured they should each have their own set. Children argue over that sort of thing, right?" I looked to Gracie and Chase for confirmation. They both nodded, looks of exhaustion flashing over their faces. The children were barely one, so I couldn't imagine them exactly arguing over things, but I'm sure they had their ways.

"That's 300 blocks."

"Yes ... is space an issue?"

"No, the issue is you're going to be their favorite if you keep buying them cool shit like that. And that's not fair."

I wanted to point out that blocks were far from 'cool shit'. Or that I hadn't even met the children nor did they know the blocks were from me. But the fact that she was picturing this one thing becoming a habit, that I would be visiting her family, bringing them gifts over and over again, made me feel warm.

"We can just tell them they're from you, dear."

Rachel's mouth opened then quickly closed. Her cheeks reddened and she looked to her sister-in-law beside me. Whatever look Gracie gave her made Rachel blush and shake her head.

"I'm going to see the babies," she mumbled, turning quickly towards a set of stairs.

"Don't you dare wake them," Gracie half whispered, half shouted as she followed after Rachel. Chase snorted at the women, but remained in the kitchen, sipping at his wine.

"If you think she's flustered now, wait till Mom gets here. There's a good reason she hasn't brought anybody home since high school. Sorry you're on the receiving end, man, but I'm gonna enjoy the show." Chase rose his glass in a mock cheers motion before downing the wine.

"Rachel said it'd be just the four of us. Plus the children."

Chase's face immediately dropped. "Oh shit."

The curse was immediately followed by heavy footsteps careening down and a blur of Rachel passed by me to crash into Chase.

"What the fuck did you tell Mom?" She'd grabbed her brother's sleeve, shaking the man as she gritted out her question. I don't think I'd ever seen her like this. Flustered and angry, like she was about to rip his arm off and fling it around wildly.

"I was just talking to her last night and said you were bringing some guy over and then ... you know, she sorta invited herself over. I meant to tell you this morning but I ... forgot."

"How could you?"

"I didn't think it was a big deal? Gracie said you've been seeing this guy for like two years."

Rachel slammed her head into Chase's shoulder, then repeated the motion over and over again. Chase leaned in and unsuccessfully whispered, "Wait, is this a different guy?"

My gut twisted. She wasn't ready for this. She wanted a relationship going somewhere but didn't want to rush to that final destination. Meeting her mom today would be too much too soon.

"It is, but it's complicated. And he's my boss," Rachel mumbled into her brother's shoulder. The man's look said it all. One way or another, me being here would make everything awkward and uncomfortable.

I stepped up and placed a gentle hand on Rachel's arm. The words stung, but I forced them out nonetheless. "I'll go. Just call me when you'd like to get picked up."

Her head sprung up, dark curls flying everywhere. She let go of her brother and took hold of my arm, her grip tight. She bit her lip, looking down for a moment before meeting my eyes. "No, I don't want you to go. It's just — it's fine. I got to deal with your mom, it's only fair you get to deal with mine."

"You're being dramatic, Rachel. Just put a baby in her arms and she'll leave you alone," Gracie huffed as she made her way back down stairs, a baby in each arm. When she reached the landing, Chase immediately crossed, taking one of the kids and kissing his wife on the cheek.

That. That was the action, the small things that I never did that made Rachel think I didn't care. This was the example of love she saw, what she expected it to look like.

I took her hand from my arm and brought it to my lips, pressing a light kiss against her knuckles. Rachel met my eyes and the strain and stress that had already started to bubble began to ease.

And then car doors slammed outside and Rachel puffed out a breath, rolling her eyes before pulling away from me. I followed her and the rest of the family out of the kitchen and into a cacophony of sharp arguments.

At the front door, three people were taking off their shoes. Rachel's mother went from arguing with her husband to chastising the younger man about how he casually kicked off his shoes and flung them in the corner. Conversation halted though when I cleared the doorway and suddenly I was the center of the attention.

So I did what I usually did for any introduction and held out my hand to the closest person, which happened to be Rachel's mother.

"Nice to meet you all. Morgan Bleckard. I'm ..." My words halted. Normally I'd describe myself based on my company, because more often than not, work was the reason why I was talking to someone in the first place. But this occasion was different, this ...

"My boyfriend," Rachel said, then, after clearing her throat, repeated, "Morgan's my boyfriend."

Chapter Seventeen

Morgan

Three months ago

Until last year, the holiday party was something I'd endured. Something I dreaded coming up. Something that I barely spent five minutes at before calling it a night.

But that wasn't the case anymore. Not when I had Rachel. Not when she walked into a room and her eyes instantly found mine.

It'd been almost two years since I met her. Two years and her entrance into the ballroom, any room, still stunned me. Her curls were pinned up, a few strands loose around her face, and her makeup was … sharper than usual. Or maybe the coloring was more distinct. Her eye color popped more, her lips shined. I wanted to ruin it, I wanted to worship her and see how long I could preserve the look, how long it would take for all her curls to fall loose.

A man stepped in her, holding out a drink for her. Rachel took the drink, smiling, toying with her hair. The man had the audacity to reach for her, hold her elbow and guide her towards where small plates were being served.

And she didn't fight it.

Reason. I needed to keep hold of reason. The man was a coworker, she was being polite. And while there wasn't a reason to hide our relationship, she might receive harassment if we flaunt it. Rachel speaking with coworkers before me was fine. *It was fine.*

Except it drove me wild. I wanted her to come to me first. I wanted to be the first one she talked to, for her to turn away others for me. And even worse, despite how unreasonable it was, I wanted to storm over there and make it clear she was mine. Grab her, kiss her, sweep her away, do something to smooth away this scratching feeling in my chest.

Then Rachel's eyes met mine and I saw some kind of understanding, like she saw my distress despite how hard I tried to hide it. She smiled, said something to the man, and crossed over to me. The tension eased so quickly, I wondered if I'd imagined it.

"Having fun, Mr. Bleckard?" she asked, holding out her plate of hors d'oeuvres. She'd gotten mostly things with cheese.

"You look gorgeous, Rachel." There was no point in answering her question, she already knew how I felt about these events. The only thing worth coming here for was her.

"Thank you, sir. You're also looking especially handsome this evening." Warm. That was the only way I could describe how Rachel made me feel.

"Don't look now, but they're taking pictures of us. Make sure to smile."

"They're supposed to be candid photos. Smiling intentionally would defeat the purpose."

"Well I guess when you put it that way." She laughed, the sound breathy. I preferred hearing her breathy voice in an entirely different situation. Perhaps it was time to bring up the room I'd booked for us upstairs.

"Oh shoot, excuse me. I just remembered my mom called on my way here and if I don't call her back, she'll assume I'm dead in a ditch." Rachel pulled out her phone from her clutch and within a few touches, was speaking with her mother. I tried not to listen too closely, tried not to mind what she said. But then she mentioned that she was with her boss and everything felt ... prickled.

It wasn't even a fair emotion. I hadn't told my mother about Rachel for my own reasons, it was likely the same for her. Except ...

As soon as Rachel hung up the call, I wrapped my arm around her and guided us towards the door.

"Already?" Rachel whispered, leaning in to me. I nodded. I couldn't name the burning, but I knew as soon as her hands were on my bare skin, it would feel better. At least I hoped so.

Chapter Eighteen

Rachel

"I 'm waiting," Gracie sang as she layered glue onto one of the invitations. I ignored her prodding, again, and instead cursed Pinterest. Normally I didn't mind a little glitter, but this was a special case. That case being Gracie was on my ass and I was still in shock from calling Morgan my boyfriend, for the first time, out loud, in front of my mother.

"I distinctly remember," Gracie continued, "You saying, and I quote, 'I'm tired of not having that.' At which point you proceeded to wave wildly at my wedding pictures on the mantel. Then said, 'I'm gonna start getting serious, I'm quitting my boss, and I'm going to settle down.' And now you're here, with said boss, *and* calling him your boyfriend. I don't think you've ever called a man your boyfriend since high school. And didn't that guy dump you because you're commitmentphobia?"

"I give up," I grumbled, tossing the invite and spilling glitter all over the kitchen counter. Whatever, Gracie can have fun picking that up later. Morgan, who sat in the living room, one of the twins asleep in his arms, gave me a look. I rolled my eyes and shook my head in a way I hoped communicated that I was just irritated. Morgan nodded and turned back to my parents who were explaining how the cruise they went on worked. I don't know what there was to explain, but Morgan nodded along politely.

"A lot's happened this week."

"Are you gonna tell me about it? Or are you just gonna walk in here next week married?" Gracie kept her voice down, but I took a worried glance at my mom. I don't know why I bothered, she's so enamored with Morgan, if I didn't know better, I'd be worried she'd try to steal him away.

"Fine. So, I went into his office on Monday and gave him my resignation letter. And –"

"Oh my god, Rachel, is that really how you were going to break up with him?" Gracie hissed under her breath, nudging me just enough to make a point without drawing attention from the other room.

"You can't break up with someone you weren't together with. I wasn't even calling him by name at that point."

"You are now."

"Yeah, well, when I gave him the letter, he got upset because he'd been under the impression that we were, like, *dating* dating."

"Oh my god, you callous bitch." Now it was my turn to nudge her. Though I definitely put a little more force behind my nudge.

"Why are you on his side? This emotional depth wasn't there a week ago. There were zero signs that our relationship was a thing."

"Dude looks at you like fucking Mr. Darcy. I don't buy that for a second."

"Didn't she think he hated her in that movie?"

Gracie was quiet for a moment and I wasn't sure if I'd gotten the right historical romance at first, but then she sighed and gestured for me to continue.

"Right, so I said I wanted to quit, he says don't, let me prove I can be what you need. I mean, I'm paraphrasing, but that was essentially it. And I didn't think he meant it at first, but the next day, he came in with flowers and asked me out on a proper date. And just ... I don't know, he made the effort to start opening up and he's been buying me shit this whole time, sorta just waiting for a reason to give me things. And ... I just didn't see how he felt about me and now I do, so yeah ... boyfriend. Sorta."

"What do you mean sorta?"

"Well, the whole thing was I wanted to start dating someone, like exclusively, to get on the path to, like, marriage. And that was all well and good with Greg, because the first step we would take would just be not seeing other people. But Greg wants kids and said I would change my mind when I told him I didn't."

"Ew," Gracie cut in.

"Yeah, I know, he can fuck right off. Clearly that wouldn't have worked, even if there was the no Morgan. And Morgan is ... so caring. I mean, he's shit at expressing it. Probably because his mom pushes toxic masculinity like it's her job. But whatever, he's clearly willing to tackle that for me. And that just sorta makes me ... panic. Like, I haven't even told Morgan I stopped things with Greg. I tried yesterday and I just ended up inviting him here instead. And with Mom, it just sorta slipped out. But like ... I don't know. I feel like I'm panicking over nothing. Which makes me feel stupid and even more anxious."

"Mmm, I felt that way before marrying Chase. The idea of calling him my husband made me gag for a while."

"What? No, it's not —"

"Yes, it is. You're getting cold feet. Just because it's not a wedding, doesn't mean you're not gonna get nervous. And just because this is something you want, something you actively took steps to get, doesn't mean you can't be nervous. It just means you're doing something new. Stoping being a stupid bitch and just tell him you wanna fuck and enjoy his riches for the foreseeable future."

"Gracie!" I nudged her under the table, she yelped and once again, everyone in the living room looked at us. This time when I met Morgan's eyes I decided it was time. No more hemming and hawing, I just had to say it and then it wouldn't be so scary.

"Fine, you win," I grumbled at Gracie before standing and mouthing at Morgan to follow me.

"I don't wanna hear shit," Gracie hissed as I walked away. I rolled my eyes but kept heading to the stairwell, not going up until I heard Morgan excuse himself and his footsteps following me. I took his hand, but kept quiet as I led him to the guest room. I had a feeling as soon as I got the first few words out, everything else would tumble out. And I'd probably jump him. So best to do that behind closed doors.

"Rachel, it's fine. You don't need to say anything," Morgan said once I'd shut the door behind us. He sat on the edge of the bed, his eyes stoic, body tense. And damn was that tension contagious. It landed hard in my gut and spread a wave of nausea. Did he realize what I was going to say? Had getting to know each other better changed his mind in the opposite direction?

"What?"

Morgan was silent for a long moment before he took a deep breath and looked away. "I know you only called me your boyfriend because that was easier than explaining our situation. I know you didn't mean it."

"Oh no, honey, that's not it at all." The relief took the breath out of me. I stepped up, nudging his foot with mine so I could stand between his legs. Morgan looked up and I ran my fingers through his short locks. There was so much emotion warring in his eyes, that my words bubbled out to fix it. "I meant it. You are my boyfriend. I mean, if that's still cool with you. I want to be with you and, you know, go get our nails done together and shit. And you don't strike me as a sports guy, but I wanna be the one you drag to games or whatever your equivalent is, even if it is just vacuuming on the weekends. And I wanna know more about you and know all your little ticks and all the things I didn't notice before. And I want —"

Morgan's hands found either side of my face, thumbs stroking my cheek, and the fumbling words stopped.

"I messed this up last time." I tried to shake my head, but Morgan held firm, thumb grazing over my lips to stop my rebuttal. "I did. I didn't ask any questions. I want to do it right this time. So ... did you speak with Greg?"

"Yeah. After … after you left on Thursday I went and said we wouldn't see each other again. He was kinda a dick about it, so, you know, bullet dodged there." He kept his thumb on my bottom lip as I talked, the pressure feather light.

"And from now on, there will be no other men or women? No dinners or dates with anyone else. Just us, right?"

"Yeah. Just us."

"And you'll tell me if you want something, if there's something I'm missing?"

"Yeah. As long as you tell me what you're thinking sometimes, what you're feeling."

"Yes, of course," Morgan breathed before pulling me close and bringing our lips together. It was soft, so soft and full of affection I actually felt butterflies. Real butterflies. Not just the sexual attraction, but affection. The two emotions burned into each other, mixing into a more intense heat that needed to be satisfied.

"Morgan," I murmured, none of the other thoughts floating around my head were capable of forming into actual words. I climbed up on the bed, a knee on either side of his hips, and grinded, hard. He grunted, hands falling to my hips, gripping tight.

"Rachel, we can't, your family's downstairs." Morgan's voice was tense and I wasn't sure if that was because he was anxious about being caught or just as needy as I was. I chose the interpretation that matched what I was feeling.

"It's fine. You know I can be quiet." I rocked into him, need pushing me harder than normal. Because now that everything was cleared up, now that there were no more obstacles, I was horny as fuck. "Are you really gonna let some other man be the last one to fuck your girlfriend?"

Suddenly the wind was knocked out of me and I was on my back. Morgan held my hands over my head, knees braced on either side of my thighs. His eyes were dark, staring me down like he was trying to decide what to do with me. And fuck, I needed him to do something soon. I was burning.

And when he didn't take any immediate action, I did. Running my leg up between his thighs and pressed against his cock.

And then he was gone.

His warmth, the hunger, all of it flickered away as he pushed off me. He made some sort of a grunt, then folded himself over on the opposite end of the bed. I waited a second for things to make sense. Then I sat up and watched as Morgan rested his head in his hands, barely covering a grimace. And then it clicked.

"Oh my god, did I hurt you?" I scrambled off the bed to stand in front of Morgan, my mind running through a list of what I could do to help. Except that list couldn't really formulate since I had no fucking clue how I could've hurt him or whatever else could possibly be wrong. I didn't press into him that hard, had I?

"Morgan, talk to me. What can I do to help?"

"Doctor. Now," he grumbled, pushing up to stand, one hand cupping his ... well his dick.

According to my phone, I'd only been in the doctor's waiting room for 20 minutes. Which wasn't a lot of time, especially when you consider the fact that Morgan probably had to wait some more after he went back to the room. But that rationale didn't calm my nerves.

In fact, I'd been on the phone with Gracie for most of the time, and she did her best to assure me that nothing could possibly be that wrong with him because he didn't need an ambulance or even to go to the ER. In fact, the office Morgan directed me to was a standard practice, one that normally wasn't even open on the weekends. And yet, there was someone there to greet us as soon as we arrived.

"Ma'am?"

I shot up, nearly tripping over my feet in the process. In front of me was an older woman, gray hair, slight wrinkles across her brow, and a white coat. Doctor. A doctor that was about to tell me what the fuck was going on with Morgan. And hopefully whatever was wrong with him wasn't one of the millions of things I saw on Google.

"Is Morgan all right?"

"Oh yes, you know how men are, especially when it concerns that area. No real damage done, just some extra swelling around the incision. You'll need to —"

"Incision? What incision?" Had something cut him? Did his zipper go rogue? Did incision mean stitches?

"From the — I'm sorry, you are Mr. Bleckard's girlfriend, right?" She looked down at the clipboard in her hand, then back up to me. "Ms. Conrad, yes?"

"Um, yeah. It's sorta new."

"Oh. Well, you are his emergency contact, but if he hasn't told you about this specific medical matter, then it's not my place to say anything." The woman bit her lip, looking down at the chart to avoid my gaze, which was probably edging on pleading.

"But he's okay, isn't he?" I stammered out. What could be so bad that she couldn't tell me?

"Oh, yes. He'll be fine with some rest and pain relievers. You can go in and see him now, he's just icing ... the wound. I would recommend refraining from any ... romantic activities for a while longer. Anyways, he's just through there, first door on your left." The doctor pointed towards the door Morgan had gone through earlier and then made her way quickly to the receptionist. I took the hint and didn't waste any time in making my way back to Morgan.

In the room, he sat hunched over. One hand held an ice patch to his groin, the other held his head, propped up on his knee. He didn't look up when I walked in, so I sat in the hard plastic chair against the wall and waited. And then waited a while longer. Normally, I didn't have a problem waiting for Morgan to gather his thoughts. But right now an irrational part of my brain was screaming *cancer, cancer, cancer*.

"Are your balls all right?" I blurted. Morgan finally looked up and his face was so pale. It was already odd enough seeing him in actual casual clothes, this look took things to a whole other level.

"Rachel, I ... kept something from you."

Oh my god, the twisting feeling was suddenly back and so much worse than before. I'd never been afraid of someone cheating on me, I hadn't exactly been in a relationship where that was technically possible, but now the thought stuck in my throat. I'd been mostly indifferent about those dinners before, but remembering them now made me sick. How had I been able to convince myself I didn't care before?

"The other day when I left early —"

"You went and saw someone, didn't you? One of those women you dated, the daddy's trust fund women. Your mother likes them, it'd make sense if you wanted them when I just misunderstood you and used you for sex this whole time. And then you just felt obligated to come with me today and say those things." My breath was coming in harsh waves. Shit, I felt so stupid and anxious and all over the place.

"What? Rachel, no. I went to get a vasectomy."

The panic thoughts stopped with a record scratch. "What?"

"I scheduled the appointment that morning, after we left your place. I wanted to get it done as soon as possible. You've never said anything about a pregnancy scare, but I figured that might've been something you thought

I wouldn't care about before and I wanted to eliminate that stressor. And it … it was something I could do for you that would show you I care."

Suddenly I could breathe normally again. "You did that after we had one conversation?"

Morgan sighed, setting aside the ice pack so he could stand and wrapped me in his arms.

"Yes. You already know I'm not one to hesitate when I make up my mind. And since you were of the same mindset, I took the necessary steps."

"You don't think I'll change my mind?"

Morgan pulled away to look at me brow furrowed. "No."

A simple answer. No qualifiers. No buts.

"Well …" Now that the irrational panic had subsided, I was at a loss of what to say. So the only thing to pop out of my mouth was, besides some giggling, "Why didn't you tell me?"

Morgan looked away. He ran his tongue across his upper lip and sighed again. Morgan was surprisingly cute when he was nervous.

"You'd mentioned that you didn't want to rush things. I didn't want my decision to do this make you think I was disrespecting that wish. I just didn't see the point in waiting either, especially with something I can do for you."

"Morgan," I cried, playfully smacking his arm. "We can't both be anxious overthinkers."

"You don't strike me as anxious."

"I am when you're hurt and you haven't told me what's wrong." I rested my head on his chest, finding comfort there.

"I'm not that hurt," he muttered.

"Morgan, you were so pale. I can't believe you let me even get on top of you in the first place." I knocked my forehead against him and he chuckled.

"I got you off of me."

"By getting on top. You should've told my horny ass to sit down."

"Well, I have a hard time saying no to you. Especially under those circumstances."

"Does that mean you'll let me take you home and take care of you?"

"And by take care of me, you mean ...?"

"Don't worry, honey, I'm not going to touch your dick. The doctor specifically said no 'romantic activities.' So we'll have to celebrate our relationship some other day."

"Hm, I'm sure there are other things we can do in the meantime." Morgan's hand slid under my chin and pulled until I was looking at him. And then his lips were on mine. It wasn't hot and heavy, or anything like our previous kisses. But it was right. And for the first time in a really long time, I felt settled.

Chapter Nineteen

Morgan

Two weeks later

"You ate your dessert awfully fast, Rachel," I noted. My girlfriend narrowed her eyes at me and I couldn't help but grin. She wasn't exactly happy with me since I decided we might as well wait until the doctor confirmed my vasectomy was successful to have sex. And since my test aligned with her birthday, I decided to make the most of it.

"I'd rather you were eating my dessert," she huffed and I chuckled.

"You think I'm not planning to do that when I get you home?" She didn't have any response for that. At least she'd always known that was a given.

"I just think it's some sort of cruel and unusual punishment that you're forcing me to wait. On my birthday, no less." It turns out Rachel enjoyed complaining. And pouting. And if I pointed it out, she'd just pout some more. Perhaps I would've found the behavior annoying, except it was Rachel. And it meant she was comfortable enough to be herself with me.

"You'll get everything you want soon enough." I flagged down our waiter and handed over my card, just as eager to get her home.

Tonight I was going to tell Rachel I loved her. I'd learned my lesson with the vasectomy incident. Keeping things from her because I was worried it'd be too much was pointless. She'd be able to tell I was holding back something and I'd just end up worrying her more.

Plus I didn't want the first time I told her to be when I was fucking her senseless. And since that was what I planned on doing tonight, I needed to tell her soon.

"Rachel?" She looked up at me, eyes meeting mine for just a moment before flickering to my mouth. She was so eager. If things go well, if I didn't ruin the mood, we might not make it back home.

"Yes?" she prompted. I could feel her leg bouncing under the table.

Just say it.

"I love you." Relief flooded me, like walking into a warm room after walking out of the cold. But then Rachel's brow furrowed.

"What?" she said, confusion painting her face. Shit.

"I love you." I repeated the words, as if they'd do anything to help the situation. I could see Rachel trying to reason out what I'd just said. But there wasn't any reason for it. That's what love was, right?

"But we've ... we've only actually been going out for a few weeks. And I —"

"We might have only been officially together these last two weeks, but that doesn't mean the time before meant nothing."

"I guess, it's just that —"

"Do you not believe me?" When I pictured telling her, I imagined a million different ways it could go wrong. What I hadn't imagined was her arguing with me, acting like she didn't even believe the words.

Rachel was quiet for a moment, her face shifting through a range of emotions. Most of which was apprehension. And then she stood, mumbled something about needing air, and headed towards the door.

I followed.

When I reached the door, she was standing on the curb, body tilted to look down the road, presumably for a taxi.

"What are you doing?"

Rachel tensed and turned back to me, sucking her lip in.

"I'm sorry, I just wanna go home and think."

"Okay, then I'm taking you."

"What ... what about your card?" She crossed her arms over her chest, her eyes downcast. She was trying to get rid of me and I wouldn't let her, couldn't.

"I can pick it up later. And I'll take you home, just ... tell me you believe me?" When she finally looked up, she looked on the verge of tears. I took her by the arm and pulled her close, wiping her tears before resting her head on my chest. "This is about your thing with needing a minute with your emotions, isn't it?" She nodded and I let out a long breath. Guess we both need some work expressing our emotions on some level. Rachel pulled back, bright eyes meeting mine.

"Are you mad at me?" Tiny. Her voice had gotten so tiny.

"Of course not." My response was immediate. And because it felt like I should, I expanded. "I'm a little frustrated things didn't go the way I planned, but I could never be mad at you. And I don't need you to be ready to say it back, either. As long as this space doesn't mean ..." I took a breath and forced the words out "As long as we're still a couple, as long as you talk to me after you've had a chance to speak, it'll be fine." I kissed the top of her head and she nodded, hands wrapping around my back and holding tight. "All right, let's get you home, dear."

Chapter Twenty

"Gracie, I fucked up!" I cried, literally cried with tears and sobs, the whole nine yards, as soon as my sister-in-law picked up the phone.

"Sorry sis, it's Chase. And before you ask, no I will not get Gracie. She was up all night with the twins and ti's her turn to sleep. So you can either tell me about this fuck up or wait until tomorrow to talk with Gracie."

I chewed at my bottom lip, considering this. Chase and I were pretty close, but I'd never told him about my guy problems. But I felt like shit for running from Morgan and needed someone to talk to and Chase was as good an option as any. At least it wasn't Owen.

"Yeah, thanks, I'd appreciate that."

I sat for a moment, trying to put everything together into words my brother would understand.

"You still there? Because if you're not gonna talk, I might fall asleep too. Word of advice, don't have twins."

"Well Morgan got a vasectomy, so that won't be a problem." The words were out of my mouth instantly, like I was rising to the bait. I guess teasing me was Chase's way of getting to talk.

"Wait, for real? Well I guess I should tell Mom to save her breath on the get pregnant to ensure a ring bit. Could see that advice just gleaming in her eyes when y'all were over."

"Mom knows I don't want kids."

"Yeah, well she's not the best listener. So tell me what you fucked up."

I shuffled in my bed, settling under covers I hadn't actually slept here in days. It'd only been two weeks, but I already pretty much lived at Morgan's place. And now my own bed felt too cold.

"Morgan told me he loved me."

"Okay and?" From across the line, I could hear Chase pouring something, probably wine. That's what Gracie and I always did when had girl talks and occasionally Chase joined us. Something about being able to picture exactly what he was doing was reassuring.

"And I panicked and said I needed time to think. And I almost walked out of the restaurant on him." On the other end, Chase snickered. "Shut up and give me some brotherly advice. What do I do? Did I just ruin everything by not saying it back right away?"

"I mean, if he actually loves you, no."

"But I totally freaked out. And I had a freak out calling him my boyfriend too."

"Oh really? Couldn't tell."

"Shut up." I shifted in bed again, kicking at the sheets.

"I'm sorry to say sis, you're probably gonna freak out about shit your whole life, just like mom."

"Excuse me!" I shot, ready to grab my keys and go fight my brother.

"I don't mean, like, you freak out the same way, but you got your anxiety from somewhere. You know? As long as you let Morgan know you need space to think through your freak out and you don't avoid the issue forever, I'm sure it'll be fine."I opened my mouth to say thank you just as Chase added, "Or maybe not. I'm not a therapist."

"Great, thanks," I mumbled.

"So ..." Chase started and when he realized I wasn't picking up on whatever he was trying to say, added, "Do you love him?"

"I don't know. But my running away from him probably isn't a good sign."

"I mean it's not a great sign, but you also did bring him over here, which is a pretty big sign that you do."

I mulled over for a minute. And then I stayed quiet because I didn't want to admit that Chase was right. I did love Morgan. And I just freaked out because it's new and apparently I was just going to always freak out about shit. Fun.

"Does it ever get less scary?"

"Does what get less scary?"

"Being in love?"

"Oh, hell yeah. Just takes a little practice, you know?"

"Practice, huh? Well, I guess I'll have to get some of that. Thank, Chase. That was actually really helpful."

"Well, I am a dad now, so I've gotta work on my sagely advice. You're a good practice dummy before I have to give advice to the twins."

"Oh thanks, I feel super loved now."

"Shut up, you are loved, dumbass."

My game plan was to tell Morgan as soon as I got in to work. Except he was already closed up in his office on a business calls by the time I got in. In fact, his whole calendar was just business call after business call. He was filling his day with work, either so he wouldn't accidentally pressure me for an answer or because he was worried I'd already found one.

And I was eager to assuage that worry.

But since I couldn't walk in on a phone call and blurt out my feelings, I settled on sending him a message. Except when I went to type it, nothing sounded good. 'Can we talk?' was way too vague and cryptic and if I was on the receiving end of that, I'd assume the worst. 'Let's do lunch,' felt too casual.

Fuck it, I'll just tell him I love him.

Within seconds of me hitting send, Morgan's door burst open.

"I take it back," he murmured as he made his way over to me, eyes wild.

"Oh, that's … fair, I guess." I tried to hide my disappointment. Of course he wanted to take it back, I couldn't even tell him I loved him immediately.

But Morgan didn't say anything, didn't even seem to register what I had said. When he reached me, he bent down, grabbing my ass and hiking me up his body. One hand slid under me, holding me close, and the other slid my leg up and around his waist. I took the hint and wrapped my other leg around him.

"Turns out I can be mad at you." What? "How dare you message me that?"

Morgan walked us back into his office and my heart started pounding. Were we about to have make up sex? I mean, we're not really making up from a fight, but it felt similar.

But when Morgan set me on his desk, one hand stayed wrapped around me and the other … went to his keyboard.

"What're you doing?"

"I'm canceling my calls for today and setting up our out of office emails so we can go home and do this right?"

"Home?"

"Yes, home. I'd like to fuck the woman that I love in the comfort of my own bed for once."

Chapter Twenty-One

Rachel

One year later

Send. There, just like Gracie was always telling me, I communicated something I was anxious about instead of letting it fester in my head. Did I communicate it the most healthy way? Not exactly, but I think Morgan would get a laugh out of it. Well, maybe not a laugh, but definitely that my girl's being silly again and I love her for it smile.

Morgan's door squeaked open and he stepped out, frowning at his phone. Probably looking at the to do list I just sent him. Most of it was work stuff. There were a lot of reports due back since it was the end of the quarter. But I'd added one other thing.

"Rachel?"

"Yes, sir?" Morgan's mouth twitched, fighting back a more feral response so he could address the real reason he came out here for.

"Why did you add 'buy an engagement ring' to my to do list?"

I straightened my shoulders. "Because I think you should buy one."

"And what makes you think I haven't?" Oh. "Why do you think we went to get our nails done?" *Oh.* "And going to Richmond next week?" Wait, that one threw me.

"I thought we were going to a conference."

"No, we're going to see —"

"The corgi breeder!" I hopped out of my chair and into Morgan's arms so fast, I almost knocked him over. But he stood firm, hugging me tight and nuzzling into my neck.

"I had a whole thing planned, dear. It was going to be very romantic," he grumbled.

"I'm sorry." I couldn't help but giggle and that got worse when Morgan swept me off my feet and carried me towards his office.

"Oh, am I in trouble, sir?" He nipped at my ear and kicked his office door closed. He turned, pressing me up against the door, and slid a hand under my skirt.

"Yes, you are, dear."

K.E. Monteith is an anxious hot mess that writes about people like her fall in love and get spicy. You'll usually find her talking about her dogs, complaining about chronic pain, or screaming about something DropOut related or her current hyper fixation.

Sign up for her newsletter for bonus scenes, giveaways, and more.

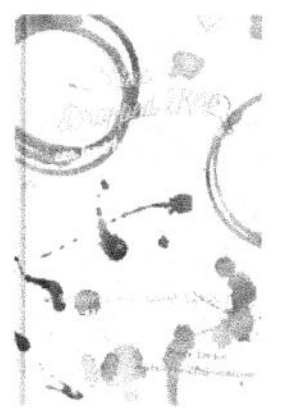